DISNEY FROZEN

POLAR NIGHTS

CAST INTO DARKNESS

POLAR NIGHTS

CAST INTO DARKNESS

AN ORIGINAL TALE BY

JEN CALONITA AND MARI MANCUSI

DISNEP PRESS
Los Angeles • New York

Printed in the United States of America
First Hardcover Edition, July 2022
1 3 5 7 9 10 8 6 4 2
FAC-004510-22154

Library of Congress Control Number: 2021949325
ISBN 978-1-368-07664-7

Illustrations by Olga Mosqueda
Design by Winnie Ho and Alfred Giuliani

Visit disneybooks.com

For the FROZEN fans:

Only Ahtohallan knows
how much we appreciate you.

—JC & MM

CHAPTER ONE

Elsa

THUMP . . .

    Thump . . .

    Thump . . .

    Queen Anna of Arendelle awoke with a start. She jerked up in bed, her heart beating madly in her chest. Her gaze darted from left to right—she pricked up her ears. The hairs on the back of her neck stood on end. What was that noise? That horrible noise? It seemed to be coming from outside, somewhere in the garden. . . .

    Thump . . .

    Thump . . .

    Thump . . .

    Anna slipped out of bed. Headed to the door. As

queen, she was responsible for keeping her people safe. Which meant she needed to investigate. Even if she was scared. Even if she was terrified at what she would find outside.

Her hand wrapped slowly around the door handle. She turned the knob—

"No, Anna! Don't do it! It's a trap! I know it's a trap!" Olaf, the talking snowman, cried out in horror.

He anxiously leapt out of his seat, somehow managing to lose both stick arms. Racing around the campfire, he bounced over Bruni—the salamander-like Fire Spirit, who had been curled up on a small pile of magical snow—and then threw himself between Anna and Sven the reindeer, who had been "telling" the tale of terror in a voice that sounded suspiciously like Kristoff's.

"Don't you hurt my Anna!" he yelled at Sven.

Sven snorted and sniffed the snowman's carrot nose. Olaf took a wary step backward, bumping into Anna and almost losing his head in the process—literally. She laughed and set it back on straight before giving it an affectionate pat.

"Don't worry, Olaf," she said comfortingly. "It's only a story."

"Also," Elsa added, retrieving Olaf's detached arms and tossing them to her sister, who reaffixed them to his body, "I'm pretty sure I know where this is going."

"Shh!" scolded Kristoff, wagging a finger at Elsa. "No spoilers!" He turned to his reindeer encouragingly. "Go ahead, Sven. They're obviously just jealous of your superior spooky storytelling skills."

Elsa couldn't suppress a small smile as she watched the reindeer give another longing look at Olaf's carrot nose, which was no longer within nibbling reach. She wondered, not for the first time, how badly Sven must wish he could talk for real, without having his buddy Kristoff "interpret" for him. Then again, Sven did a pretty good job of letting everyone know what he was feeling without having to speak a word. Even if that feeling was just concern over where his next carrot to munch on might be coming from.

Olaf sighed and retreated back to his seat on the log next to Elsa. She gave him a comforting squeeze, then looked around the campfire circle, her heart suddenly feeling very full. The Enchanted Forest camping trip had been her idea, and she was thankful her sister, Anna, had found the time to get away from her queenly duties for a night to join her. Elsa knew all too well that being queen of Arendelle was a full-time job. After all, it had been her position for years before Anna took over two months earlier. She was proud of her younger sister for taking it all on without a complaint. In fact, Anna seemed to enjoy the challenge. And Elsa knew the people of Arendelle loved Anna as much as she loved them.

But that was nothing compared to the love between these two sisters. Even though they now lived apart, they both made sure they were never too busy to spend time together regularly, either in the Enchanted Forest like they were now, or for weekly family game nights back in Arendelle, which still felt like a second home to Elsa. (Anna had even let Elsa keep her bedroom, which had once been their mother and father's, knowing how much it meant to her sister.) And, starting the next day, Elsa was planning to spend an extended holiday in Arendelle to help Anna prepare for her very first Polar Nights celebration as queen.

The Polar Nights festivities came once a year to Arendelle around the time of the winter solstice—and Elsa's birthday! It was a time when the land was wrapped in perpetual twilight, the sun never fully rising for an entire week. But it wasn't dull or too dark, like it could be in some kingdoms further to the north. Instead, the Arendellian skies were bathed in a beautiful dusky blue haze with plenty of light to see by. Some years, if they were lucky, they would even be treated to breathtaking views of the Northern Lights themselves, the aurora borealis painting the sky in brilliant emerald green.

Once upon a time, according to the history books, people had been frightened by the Polar Nights phenomenon, believing the sun had died and that the world would soon expire along with it. But now they knew this was only a temporary pause. Soon the sun would rise again, like a phoenix from the ashes, and life would begin anew.

But in the meantime, it was a great excuse to party.

It was also a time of migration for the Northuldra. No longer stuck in the Enchanted Forest, they were looking forward to journeying across the land, leading their reindeer to new and fertile pastures. So Elsa had said her temporary goodbyes to her new friends as they headed north, assuring them she'd see them soon.

After all, even the Snow Queen needed a little rest and relaxation every once in a while.

She turned back to Kristoff and Sven, realizing they were continuing their story.

Anna crept quietly out of the house and into the gardens beyond. It was dark—so dark she could not see her hands in front of her face—and she held her breath as she walked, too fearful to even make a sound. Suddenly, lightning flashed from the sky, illuminating the field in front of her. Anna gasped at what she saw. Or rather, what she didn't see. And suddenly she realized what night this truly was: the night she thought would never come.

Sven drummed his hooves against the ground dramatically. Olaf's eyes grew wide with fright. He cuddled a little closer to Elsa.

"The night . . . the night completely . . . the night completely without . . ." Kristoff teased.

"Hope?" Olaf squeaked. "*Life?* A slim but real chance for a better tomorrow?"

"Or maybe . . . carrots?" Elsa suggested wryly.

"*Carrots!*" Sven/Kristoff roared after giving Elsa a scolding look. "It was *the night without carrots.*"

Olaf screeched in horror, grabbing his nose protectively. Sven snorted while Kristoff guffawed in glee.

Elsa rolled her eyes. "A night without carrots," she deadpanned. "How . . . terrifying."

"Oh, please! That's not terrifying! That's not even remotely scary!" Anna protested, looking a lot more annoyed by the silly twist in the tale than she probably had any right to be. She shook her head, her copper-colored locks swinging from side to side. "I mean, so what? No carrots! We could just eat broccoli instead. Or lettuce. Or chocolate." She pursed her lips. "Now, a night without chocolate. *That* would be scary." She poked Kristoff playfully in the arm. "Which is why I'm really hoping you didn't forget our—"

"Choco-versary," Kristoff finished with a grin. He slung his arm around Anna's shoulders and pulled her close. "Come on now. Give me a little credit. How could

I possibly forget the sixth anniversary of our very first time eating chocolate together? I mean, it's downright historic. By all rights, it should be added to the annals of Arendelle history someday!"

Anna beamed. Meanwhile, Elsa couldn't help emitting a small snort. *Choco-versary.* How ridiculously cute could one couple be? Even though Kristoff drove her crazy sometimes, she had to admit he was the perfect match for her sister. She couldn't wait for them to get married someday and have little Annas and Kristoffs running around Arendelle. She was definitely planning on being the cool aunt. Literally.

Anna leaned against Kristoff, looking up at him with wide, overly innocent blue eyes. "And to celebrate this momentous, historical occasion, you're going to . . . ?"

Kristoff shook his head, pushing her back upright. "Nope. Not a chance. Good try, though."

Anna groaned. "No fair," she said, pretending to be grumpy. "We're engaged now, which means there should be no secrets between us."

"He's not keeping a secret!" Olaf piped in helpfully. "He just hasn't come up with anything yet!"

"Olaf!" Kristoff cried. "You weren't supposed to —"

"Wait, what?" Anna cried in mock horror. "You don't have a plan for our Choco-versary yet? It's less than a week away!"

"I know," Kristoff assured her, shooting Olaf a deadly look. "I'm just deciding which of my epic anniversary ideas is the right one to move forward with. I want to make sure everything is absolutely perfect for the love of my life, that's all." He reached for her hand, pressing his mouth against her palm.

"Oh." Anna pursed her lips, as if trying to decide if he was teasing or not. "I guess that makes sense. . . ."

Elsa stifled a laugh, deciding it was time for a subject change before poor Kristoff got in any more trouble. "How are the preparations for the Polar Nights festivities going?"

Anna sat up straight, all thoughts of chocolate visibly stampeding out of her head. This was her favorite topic these days. "Oh, they're going amazing!" she declared. "I've planned all sorts of activities: ice-carving contests, reindeer racing . . . and dance parties! So many dance parties!"

"I can't wait," Elsa said. "I know it's going to be great."

"I'm just glad you're coming," Anna said, smiling at her sister. "And just think! This year we'll have the Spirits to help, too!" She turned to Bruni, who had gone back to lounging on a rock. "Are you going to help us light our bonfires, little one?"

Bruni bounced up and down, sparks of purple flame sputtering from its back, clearly excited about the task. Elsa smiled and beckoned to the Fire Spirit. It leapt into her lap and curled up happily as she stroked it with an icy finger, helping it cool down again.

"Sounds amazing. Sure to be the best week ever. Now can we get back to the scary stories?" Olaf begged, bouncing on his log. "I've got the best one! It's all about Samantha and her—"

"Sorry, Olaf," Kristoff interjected. "But it's my turn, actually."

"Uh, didn't you just have a turn?" Anna asked.

"Nope. That was Sven, remember?" Kristoff said with a mischievous grin.

"Oh. Right." Anna snorted. "*Sven* told the story."

"And it was the best story ever!" Kristoff declared in Sven's voice. The reindeer, who was standing beside him, just rolled his eyes.

"By all means, Kristoff," Elsa said with an impish smile, "go right ahead."

"Why, thank you, your Snow Queen-ness," Kristoff replied, clearing his throat. He leaned forward, his blue eyes shining brightly in the firelight. "Okay, here's my tale, which I once heard from the ice harvesters I worked with when I was growing up. But be warned, it is truly terrifying. Horribly horrific. Younger viewers"—he glanced knowingly at Olaf—"might want to leave the campfire."

Olaf huffed, crossing his arms in front of his chest. "Please. As long as it's not about carrots, I'll be fine."

Kristoff shrugged. "Don't say I didn't warn you." He turned back to the two sisters. "You see, this isn't just any old story. It's actually true. It happened not very far from Arendelle, either. In fact, it happened on this very night, fifty years ago today."

Elsa leaned forward, curious despite herself. "Oh, yeah?"

"You know the kingdom of Vesterland, right?"

"Of course. That's King Jonas and his daughter Princess Mari's kingdom," Anna replied, naming her friends who lived in a neighboring land. She and Mari had become great buddies a few years earlier, and they still kept in touch.

Kristoff nodded. "Right. But, you see, it wasn't always theirs. Once upon a time, it belonged to two sisters. Two princesses, to be precise."

"Hmm . . ." Elsa said with a smile. "Sounds vaguely familiar."

"Actually, no." Kristoff shook his head. "These princesses were nothing like you and Anna. In fact, they did not get along at all. The younger sister, Inger, hated her older sister, Sissel. Sissel, you see, had everything that Inger always wanted. Sissel was beautiful. She was kind. She was special in every way. She was to be Vesterland's future queen when she came of age. And Inger, well, she was . . ."

"Completely ordinary?" Olaf guessed. Anna shot him an impatient look.

"Consumed with jealousy," Kristoff corrected. "She wanted nothing more than to get rid of her older sister so she could ascend the throne herself."

"Unlike me!" Anna broke in. "I thought Elsa made an amazing queen. Not that I wasn't fine with taking over for her, of course. We're both exactly where we should be now." She threw a smile to her sister. Elsa smiled back, reaching across to squeeze Anna's hand.

Kristoff groaned. "Can I get back to my scary story now?"

"Please do! It's absolutely riveting so far!" Olaf declared. He was sitting on the edge of his log.

"Why, thank you, Olaf," Kristoff said. He leaned in again. "Well, one day, Inger got her wish. While on a trip to Arendelle, she caught her sister standing by the rushing river—alone. Seeing her moment, Inger snuck behind her and shoved her in! Sissel struggled to swim, but the current was too strong. She screamed for help, begging her sister to save her. But Inger only laughed at her, watching with cruel glee as Sissel went over a huge waterfall and drowned."

"Whoa!" Anna burst out. "*So* not where I thought this was going!" Kristoff shot her a look. "Oh . . . sorry." She clamped a hand over her mouth. "Please continue."

Kristoff clasped his hands together. "Well, after that, Inger thought she had won. That she would go back home and take her sister's place as queen. But someone witnessed her evil deed and reported it back to your grandfather, King Runeard. He arrested Inger and put her on a prison ship. She was to be banished from Arendelle—and Vesterland—forever."

"Our grandfather doing something just and good? That's . . . unexpected," Elsa remarked dryly, raising an eyebrow.

After all, their grandfather hadn't exactly been a model king during his reign. Power hungry, fearmongering, yes. Not to mention all the harm he'd done to the Northuldra, their mother's people, by deceiving them into supporting his dam project, which would dry up their lands and destroy their way of life.

"Right? But, sadly, Sissel never got justice. The prison ship Inger was on went down at sea before it could ever reach its destination," Kristoff declared with a dramatic flourish. "And Inger—like her sister—also drowned."

"Well!" Olaf piped up. "That story was indeed terrifying. Okay, Kristoff. You win. Perhaps we can toast marshmallows now?" He looked hopefully at the group.

"Hold on, Olaf. That's not the end of my story," Kristoff scolded. "In fact, it's only the beginning. Because Sissel, you see, didn't really die. Or at least she didn't *stay* dead. Instead, she came back as a horrible creature known as a draugr."

Something about the word sent an involuntary shiver down Elsa's spine. She felt a slight shift in the wind, and goose bumps formed on her arm. She tried to smooth them down with her hand. "A draugr? What's a draugr?" she asked, even though she wasn't entirely sure she wanted to know.

Anna raised her hand eagerly. "Ooh! I know! I know!" she cried. "I read all about them in this book I found in the secret room in the castle library. They're creatures of old folklore, and they supposedly cause terrible storms when they show up. People used to blame them when the weather got bad."

Kristoff nodded approvingly. "That's exactly right."

"You're so smart," Elsa teased, poking Anna. Anna shrugged sheepishly.

"And so the evil draugr who used to be sweet Sissel began to roam the land," Kristoff continued, "leaving havoc in its wake. No longer human, no longer kind or good. It was now nothing more than a soulless monster ready to seek revenge against those who did it wrong."

"Moral of the story? Always be nice to your sister," Anna concluded. She grinned at Elsa. "Got it!"

Elsa smiled back at her, though for some reason she

still felt a little uneasy. Maybe because it was such an unsettling story. Or perhaps it was the fact that she hadn't always been the best sister herself. She tried to imagine Anna coming back as an evil monster to seek revenge, but couldn't exactly picture it. Mostly because the only monstrous thing about Anna was her appetite for chocolate.

"So where is the draugr now?" Olaf asked, his eyes still wide and terrified. "You said this story was true. Does that mean the draugr's still out there somewhere?"

"Of course it is," Kristoff replied, turning his attention back to the snowman. His thick eyebrows furrowed. He lowered his voice by a menacing octave. "And it's said that if you tell its story—especially tonight, the night it all happened—you will awaken it from its slumber and it will rise again, renewing its never-ending quest for revenge."

Kristoff raised his arms in front of him, casting dark shadows across Olaf's frightened face. "So, my little snowman friend, the next time the skies grow dark . . . or the rain begins to fall . . . beware. Because it could be a simple storm. Or it could be Sinister Sissel, lurking just behind you in the shadows. Ready to—"

CRACK!

Suddenly thunder boomed from above. Lightning streaked across the sky. Olaf screamed, leaping into Elsa's arms.

"The draugr! It's Sinister Sissel!" he cried. *"She's come to get us all!"*

CHAPTER TWO

Anna

ANNA WATCHED AS ELSA GENTLY SET the panicked snowman back down. "Olaf, it's just a storm coming," she assured him. A moment later there was a second flash of lightning, followed by a roll of approaching thunder. "Not some monster from a story."

Olaf glanced nervously up at the sky. "You sure about that? The timing here feels a bit coincidental."

"Yes, Kristoff was only telling a story," Anna said soothingly, shooting the ice harvester a look. "And, clearly, he wins for scariest." She checked the sky again. "But we should get into our tents."

"Because of the draugr?" Olaf whispered.

"Because of the *rain*," Elsa reassured him, holding out a hand. "I'm already feeling drops."

"But we didn't even get a chance to roast marshmallows!" Sven said, courtesy of Kristoff.

"Sorry, guys." Anna ruffled the reindeer's fur. "We'll save them for next time." Then she stood up on tippytoes to kiss Kristoff. "Now, get a good night's sleep and try not to scare each other too much with your tales of terror."

"Ooh! That's right! It's my turn!" Olaf's eyes widened. He waddled over to Kristoff and Sven. "Hey, have you guys ever heard about the time I lost my bottom half for three hours? Now that's a scary story. . . ."

"See you guys in the morning!" Anna said as she watched the boys head off to their larger tent, which was big enough to hold the reindeer. Then she turned to Elsa and grinned. "Girl time! I mean, sister time!"

Anna loved when it was the five of them playing charades, having dinner together, or engaging in lively discussions, like the answer to the question *What's the best season in Arendelle?* (Fall! No, summer! Maybe spring? Then again, winter was lovely, too—as long as it wasn't *eternal* winter. . . .) But as much as she enjoyed being with Kristoff, Sven, and Olaf, who felt entirely like family, there was something special about one-on-one time with Elsa, too.

"Is it wrong I'm secretly excited that we get a whole night to ourselves to just talk?" Anna wondered aloud. "Or do I sound like Olaf?"

"You sound like *Anna*," Elsa said with a small smile. She stood up and used her ice magic to douse the fire, which was dimming in the rain. "And no, it's not wrong. I love when it's just the two of us sometimes as well."

They grinned at each other, then felt the raindrops falling fatter and faster and quickly grabbed their things. Elsa scooped up Bruni and they ran to their tent, then closed themselves inside just as the storm arrived, thunder booming and rain coming down in buckets. The drops pelted the tent, sounding like the Earth Giants bowling, but inside Anna thought things were cozy and warm (partially because Bruni could brighten up the tent with its Fire Spirit flames).

"Olaf is not going to be able to sleep a wink, is he?" she mused as she curled up under the reindeer-hide blankets and nestled into the pillows.

"Seems unlikely," Elsa agreed as she checked to make

sure the tent ties were secure. "Poor Olaf. Or should I say, poor Kristoff and Sven."

"Maybe Kristoff and Sven can try serenading him with a lullaby." Anna pictured her fiancé, Olaf, and Sven cuddled up tight with Kristoff's lute for entertainment. "They've been working on something they call 'The Ballad of the Persnickety Proprietor.' I suspect it's about Oaken's sauna."

"Nothing says 'sleep tight' like a song about a sauna," Elsa joked, settling in beside her sister under the warm hides.

The wind was picking up, making the tent blow a bit in the breeze, but Anna knew it would hold firm. Still, she snuggled against her sister, saying the words they'd heard their mother say a thousand times before bed when they were children: "Now cuddle close. Scooch in. And tell me everything you've been up to."

"Since when? Last Friday's game night at the castle?" Elsa teased.

"That was *days* ago!" Anna said indignantly. "You've probably done a gazillion amazing things since then!"

"Which I talk about in my daily letters you get from Gale," Elsa reminded her.

"I know! But letters are different from actual talking." Anna placed her head against Elsa's. "Our letters are all about silly things like Olina's latest recipe for lingonberries or where I can find Father's book on that headstrong mermaid who decided she wanted to be human just because she met a good-looking prince. Or questions, like 'What's a five-letter word for ice?' "

"Frost!" Elsa burst out.

Anna knew Elsa was trying to be funny, but she also wasn't about to let her big sister shove her feelings aside. She might have been the younger sibling, but she felt protective of Elsa after all Elsa had been through the last few years. "I just want to make sure you're doing okay," she said quietly.

"I'm doing better than okay. I'm great," Elsa promised. She looked at Bruni, whose flames illuminated the small patch of snow that kept him cool. "I've been learning so much from the spirits, Honeymaren, Ryder, and all the Northuldra about the ways of the forest. And my trips to Ahtohallan have been"—Elsa looked too overwhelmed to even put her experiences with the magical river that contained memories of the past into words—"truly magical."

Anna beamed. This was exactly what she wanted to hear. "I'm so happy for you, Elsa. So, you've been learning more about your powers?"

"Yes, I'm even working on new ways to bring up memories. It's really—"

Lightning lit up the whole tent, causing Bruni to snort in excitement. For a moment, Elsa looked startled, and then she shook her head. "But enough about me," she said. "What I really want to talk about is how *you're* doing. How do you like all your new duties?"

"Me?" Anna's head popped up from the pillow. She knew Elsa was trying to change the subject, but she was going to give her a pass this time. She'd been wanting to talk to Elsa about the kingdom anyway. "I love them! All of them. Being queen and working with the people of Arendelle to make the kingdom a better place is magical, too. It feels so satisfying getting stuff done, you know?"

She started to tick off tasks on her fingers. "This week alone, I had Mr. Aldring make a new clock to give as a welcome present to the queen of Chatho when she visits next month, did a ribbon-cutting ceremony at a new shop in the village, and also sat in on a three-hour meeting about soil!"

"Let me guess—with Oskar Anders?" Elsa asked with a groan. "So painful, right?"

"Actually, it was riveting!" Anna gushed. "He was going on and on about how Arendelle's soil is the richest in all the connected kingdoms." She shook her head, remembering. "Just fascinating stuff, really! I could have listened to him all day!"

Elsa snorted. "And this is why you make such a good queen," she teased.

"I'm trying," Anna said modestly. "Though it's not always easy. At least I have Mattias. He's been such a great help. Especially with the whole pirate thing." She made a face.

Elsa sat up. "Pirate thing? This is new."

"Oh." Anna waved a hand. "It's probably not a big deal. It's just that some pirate ships have been rumored to be lurking just off Arendelle's coast for about a week now. Supposedly helmed by a legendary pirate queen they call Old Blue Eyes. They haven't done anything bad or given our ships trouble, so I guess that's good. I'm just worried they're going to try to pull something right before the festival, you know? Like I don't have enough to deal with. Anyway, Mattias assures me he's got his eye on them. And I trust him to take care of things."

"I wish he had been around when I was queen," Elsa said, thinking back to the dashing lieutenant—now a general—who had been stuck in the Enchanted Forest for so many years. He'd been a friend to their father when Agnarr was a child. Now he split his time between protecting Arendelle, advising Anna, and . . . well . . . courting his girlfriend, Halima. The two of them had been thick as thieves ever since he returned to the kingdom, and Elsa and Anna had both made bets on how quickly they would tie the knot.

"I'm not sure what I would do without him," Anna agreed. "It's nice to have help in the castle. You know, because running the kingdom is such a big task and all."

"Oh, I remember," Elsa assured her. "It's more than a job. It's a lifestyle."

"Right? And I'm always worried I'm forgetting something important that needs to be done. Or that things are going to go wrong and it'll be my fault," Anna said, stressed, the words now tumbling out of her mouth before she could stop them. "Like with the Polar Nights!

What if the ice sculptures of Aren of Arendelle end up looking like Flemmingrad the troll? Or the band forgets to show up?" Now that she was worrying, she was on a roll and couldn't stop. Not that she wanted to bring it up, but Elsa's birthday fell during the Polar Nights, too—on the winter solstice! She was secretly planning a party on the final night of the festival for her sister. *If* she could get it all done in time. "What if everything I have planned is a huge flop?"

"It's all going to work out okay. I promise," Elsa said. "And you have me at your disposal, don't forget. I'll help you, too."

Anna knew her sister was right, but she still felt worried. She just had to concentrate on happy thoughts, like Elsa being back in the castle. "It's just that this is my first festival as queen, and I want the people to enjoy themselves. I want *you* to enjoy yourself! You've been working so hard."

Elsa put her hand over Anna's. "So have you, and the people of Arendelle know that. You're a great leader, Anna. You're juggling a million different tasks at the same time, and look at you—you still have a smile on your face."

Anna raised an eyebrow.

Elsa laughed. "Okay, maybe not at this very second. But you know what I mean. Arendelle is lucky to have you. I'm so proud of you."

Anna put her free hand on top of Elsa's. "And I'm proud of you! The forest and spirits are lucky to have you." She cocked her head to one side. "If only Mother and Father could see us now, huh?"

The thought made each of them quiet, the only sound the rain pelting their tent. Anna couldn't help imagining, and not for the first time, what their world would be like if their parents were still around to watch her ascend the throne and to witness a self-assured Elsa using her powers for all the kingdom to see. But all they had were memories.

"You know," Elsa suddenly spoke up, "I remember one Polar Nights festival as a child when the weather was so warm, there wasn't enough snow to make the traditional courtyard ice sculpture."

Anna looked at her, aghast. *"No."*

"Yes." Elsa nodded. "It had been a particularly warm fall, and it just didn't feel like the start of winter yet. You were little, but I remember Father panicking. 'How can it be a Polar Nights party without an ice sculpture?' I offered to make one, but, of course, they didn't want to risk me revealing my powers. So Mother took matters into her own hands and decided to have someone carve a sculpture out of something other than ice."

"What did they use?" Anna asked, riveted as she always was when Elsa recalled a memory of their parents that she did not have.

Elsa started to laugh. "They used cheese!"

"Cheese?" Anna snorted. "I didn't realize you could carve cheese!" She stopped laughing and thought for a moment. "Wow, this changes everything."

"Yep," Elsa confirmed, sitting up now, too. "But it gets better! Mother thought it would be fun to surprise Father with the sculpture, so she had it made in secret. She told me, but we kept it from you, of course."

Anna shrugged. "I can't say I blame you. I would have blabbed. What kind of cheese did they use?" All this food talk was making her hungry. She really wished they'd had a chance to toast marshmallows.

"I think it was cheddar or Gouda or some semihard cheese. It was carved into the Arendelle coat of arms. It was beautiful!" Elsa gushed. "Mother kept it hidden in the kitchen so Father wouldn't see it, but there was one problem." Elsa started to laugh, making it harder to understand her. "Father got hungry in the middle of the night, went down to the kitchen, and . . ."

"No!" Anna interrupted, laughing so hard she had to cover her mouth. Bruni was looking from her to Elsa with interest. "He didn't! Tell me he didn't!"

"He did!" Elsa cried. "He cut off a whole piece of the crest and ate it! When Mother came down the next morning, she was horrified. I remember she was actually a little mad and said, 'What did you think this was for?' And Father said something like 'Dinner?'"

The two of them threw their heads back, laughing.

"I wish I could remember that," Anna said wistfully.

"Hmm. Maybe I can show it to you. . . ." Elsa pushed back the reindeer hide and stood up, her head touching the top pole of the tent.

Anna watched as her sister seemed to concentrate on her magic. She could only imagine what Elsa's ice memory would look like. Anna pictured Father and Mother standing over the table with the half-eaten coat of arms made from cheese, and Father's guilty look as he realized he was busted. As Elsa swirled her arms around, Anna saw ice begin to form . . . then disappear in a plume of mist.

Anna cocked her head. "What happened?" It wasn't like Elsa's magic to just fizzle out like that.

Elsa frowned, looking upset. "I don't know," she murmured. "I mean, I had it. The memory was right there, but then . . ." She trailed off and then shrugged, giving her sister an apologetic look. "I'm sorry, Anna. Even now that I've taken my place among the spirits, magic isn't always easy."

Anna pulled Elsa into a hug. "Neither is being queen, but we'll both get there."

They stood there for a moment, each listening to the thunder continue to crash, the wind whistle, and the rain pounding on the tent's roof. For a moment, Anna felt like they were the only two people in the world. As long as they had each other's backs, she knew they'd be okay.

Suddenly, though, a giant clap of thunder made both of them jump.

"Wow, this is some storm!" Anna commented, watching the top of the tent continue to ripple.

"It can't go on for much longer," Elsa guessed, "but it

is a rough one." She dropped back to her knees, settling the reindeer hide over her lap. Anna joined her, wondering if they were ever going to get any sleep.

It was then that she heard something. Or at least she thought she heard something. The faintest of sounds, but one that definitely didn't sound like the wind or rain.

In fact, it sounded a lot like someone . . . moaning.

"Do you . . . hear something?" she asked Elsa nervously.

"Um, you mean besides the deafening rainstorm outside our tent?"

Anna shook her head. Right. Of course there was nothing. It was just her mind playing tricks on her. Clearly, she was still spooked after Kristoff's silly story.

But then it came again: the moan so low it seemed to go right through her. And it sounded a little closer this time. Anna involuntarily pulled the covers up to her chin.

"Are you okay?" asked Elsa as she peered at her worriedly.

"Yeah! Of course! I'm totally fine," Anna insisted,

shoving the covers back down in embarrassment. "Sorry. I'm sure it was just—"

Her words, however, were cut off by a sudden ear-piercing scream.

CHAPTER THREE

Elsa

THE TENT FLAPS FLEW OPEN and a breathless Olaf ran in, water spraying off his body, his stick arms flying.

"The draugr! It's real! And it's here!" He catapulted himself at the two sisters, who caught him and held him jointly.

Elsa gave him a look. "Olaf, we've been through this. There is no draugr—it's just the storm, and—"

Two more figures barreled into the tent, making it entirely too tight to even move.

"Olaf isn't joking," Kristoff said, breathing as hard as if he'd just run a mile. "There's something out there.

Sven and I both saw it!" Sven nodded, shivering in his wet coat.

Elsa felt the briefest of chills go through her body, and it had nothing to do with the blast of icy air blowing through the tent now that the flaps were rippling free in the wind. The storm was so intense she couldn't even see the boys' tent, which was only a few feet away. "You guys aren't just trying to scare us, are you?" she asked, half hoping it was the case.

"Yeah, 'cause we don't scare easily, you know," Anna piped in, puffing out her chest a little. "I mean, I've faced down deadly wolves, bad boyfriends . . . not to mention gigantic snow monsters created by my own sister to throw me out of her icy fortress of solitude!"

Elsa shot an apologetic look at Anna. Not her best sisterly moment, for sure. "Look," she said, prying Olaf off her and setting him down on the ground, "I'm sure you were just spooked by the story Kristoff told. And then the wind blew in a weird way, and—"

"No," Kristoff stated firmly, his chest still rising and falling fast. "It wasn't just the wind. There was a shadow, too. A shadow that was definitely not wind-shaped. Right, Sven?"

Sven demonstrated by waving his front hooves menacingly in the air. They caught the flicker of Bruni's light, casting eerie shadows on the tent's walls. Elsa felt a shimmer of unease swim through her stomach.

"And then there was the moaning," Olaf added. "A lot of evil-sounding moaning."

"I thought I heard moaning, too," Anna mused, looking at Elsa worriedly. "Just before the boys came in."

"The wind can moan," Elsa tried, feeling as if she were grasping at straws. She wanted to keep everyone calm, but even she was admittedly starting to get a little creeped out. She tried to tell herself that the spirits of the Enchanted Forest would never let anything harm her or her family. But even Bruni was starting to act a little nervous, darting from one end of the tent to the other.

"Look, we're not messing around." Kristoff glanced back out into the storm, and the others followed his gaze. "I'm telling you, something or someone is out there."

"Not just any something! A draugr!" Olaf insisted. "Just like in the story!" He tried to hide behind Sven. "I think it wants to eat us alive!"

Elsa drew in a breath, resigning herself to the

inevitable. It wasn't that she believed there was really some draugr out in the woods. But something was going on, and she was positive no one was going to get any sleep if they didn't get some answers. She crawled over to the tent's entrance.

"Where are you going?" demanded Anna, looking concerned.

"I'm going to investigate."

"Not without me, you aren't!"

Elsa sighed. "You'll get soaked."

"I'm happy to get soaked if it saves you from becoming draugr dinner," Anna shot back.

Elsa groaned. *Here we go again.* She loved her little sister's bravery, but she worried it would be her downfall someday. "Anna—" she started.

"Look, we'll all go," Kristoff declared.

"All?" Olaf squeaked, clearly not comfortable with this suggested plan.

"All *humans*," Kristoff clarified, patting him on the head. "Olaf, we need you and Sven to guard the tent."

Sven huffed, giving Kristoff an indignant look. Kristoff shrugged apologetically.

Elsa stepped toward the tent entrance, squinting out into the rain. "Ready?" she asked, not entirely sure if she was asking Kristoff and Anna—or herself.

"Born ready!" Anna proclaimed, evidently not having the same misgivings. She pushed past Elsa without hesitation, stumbling into the rainy night. Elsa shook her head, then scrambled after her, Kristoff hot on her heels.

The sky boomed a menacing greeting as they stepped out into the elements. It was pouring so hard it was practically impossible to see. Elsa waved a hand, creating an icy canopy across two trees, and the three of them dove for cover. Once underneath, Elsa drew in a breath, trying to regain her bearings, and spotted the boys' tent. She inhaled sharply. Kristoff, Sven, and Olaf's tent had been completely knocked down, which could have been explained by the wind. Except . . .

"Are those . . . claw marks?" Elsa asked, shouting to be heard over the wind. Her eyes traveled up the sides of the tent, where it looked as if it had been sheared by a knife. She glanced at Kristoff. "Did something attack your tent?"

"I don't know." Kristoff looked as baffled as she felt. "When we heard the moaning and saw the shadow, we ran to your tent." He paused, then squared his shoulders. "I mean, just to make sure you guys were okay and all. Not 'cause we were scared."

"Of course, honey," said Anna as she comforted him, putting a supportive hand on his back. Then she turned to Elsa. "Maybe the tent caught on a tree branch."

"Maybe," Elsa said. Her eyes rose up to scout the forest behind the tent. But the tent wasn't close enough to any trees to have gotten tangled in the branches.

She bit her lower lip uneasily. She didn't believe for a second it could be a monster out of a spooky story, but at the same time it had to be something. *A wolf?* Wolves were smart enough not to be out in this mess. Also, they were usually only after food—and yet there was a whole plate of leftover *grillpolser* they'd cooked over the fire for dinner sitting on a nearby log. Soaked, but definitely still edible by wolf standards.

But what else could it be?

She lifted her eyes to the sky and sang a few notes. A moment later, Gale whipped in, swirling around them in question. The storm, of course, didn't bother the Wind Spirit one bit.

"Can you go and look around?" Elsa asked it. "See if you see anything out of the ordinary?"

Gale swept up and out, disappearing into the darkness. Elsa shrugged and turned to her sister and Kristoff. "If anything's out there, Gale will find it," she assured them.

Anna shivered. Kristoff put his arm around her, holding her close. "Are you okay?" he asked.

"I'm fine!" Anna protested, surprising Elsa by pushing him away with more force than necessary. "I'm just freezing! And soaking wet, too." She scowled. "Why are we out here again?"

Elsa frowned. "I never said you had to come," she reminded her sister. "You could have stayed in the tent with Olaf and Sven."

"The tent . . ." Kristoff's eyes fell to his collapsed tent. "Wait! What happened to my tent?"

"Excuse me?" Elsa turned to him, really confused now. "What are you talking about?"

"It's . . . ruined. My beautiful tent. And . . . is that a

tear down the side of it? I just paid that off, you know!" He glanced accusingly at Anna, who shrugged back at him like she had no idea what he was talking about.

A small worry fluttered in Elsa's stomach. She looked from Kristoff to Anna, who looked back at her in confusion. Were they just playing around? If so, it wasn't funny.

"Look, why don't you two get back to our tent. Check on Olaf and Sven," she said, trying to swallow down her concern. "I'll wait for Gale to return."

She expected Anna to argue, but to her surprise, her sister nodded vacantly, taking Kristoff by the arm and leading him back to the tent. They crawled inside, pulling the flaps closed behind them. Elsa shook her head. *That was weird, right?*

But she didn't have time to dwell on it. For at that moment Gale returned, swirling around her and tickling her ears.

"Anything?" she asked. But the Wind Spirit moved Elsa's skirt from side to side, the spirit's version of saying *nope*. Elsa sighed.

"Okay, then," she replied. "It must have been the wind. And maybe it blew some tree branches down, which caused the tent to tear." It didn't seem likely, but she was out of explanations. And everything seemed quiet now; even the storm was starting to subside. Whatever it was, it was gone. Her shoulders slumped in relief.

"Thanks, Gale," she said to the spirit. "I'll see you in the morning. Remember, we're going to Arendelle tomorrow!"

Gale swept up a big pile of wet leaves in excitement. The Wind Spirit loved going to Arendelle, especially now that Anna had commissioned that beautiful statue of their parents in the town square. Gale loved to spend hours swirling around the sculpture of Queen Iduna. They clearly had been special friends back when their mother was young. If only the Wind Spirit could talk. Elsa was sure it had so many wonderful stories. She wondered, not for the first time, if Gale missed her mother as much as she did.

After saying goodbye to the spirit, Elsa made her way to the tent that was still intact. The rain had stopped completely now, but she was wet and freezing, not to mention wide awake from the whole crazy saga. With that, and the fact that there were now five bodies sharing their tiny tent, she was pretty sure none of them would get much sleep.

But to Elsa's surprise, when she crawled back into the tent, all she heard was snoring. Olaf, Sven, Kristoff, and Anna were all snuggled up under the reindeer hides—with Olaf using Sven's body as a pillow.

They were all peacefully asleep. As if nothing had happened at all.

CHAPTER FOUR

Anna

IN THE MORNING, the world looked brighter. At least, that's what Anna was thinking as she emerged from their crowded tent. She had a crick in her neck from contorting like a pretzel to squeeze in next to Olaf and Sven, but at least the rain had stopped. In fact, the skies were bright blue—and the sun was shining happily down on them. Which meant it was time to go! The days were shorter leading up to the Polar Nights, and Anna didn't want to miss a moment of the light to work by.

"Rise and shine, beauties!" Anna yelled into the tent, louder than was necessary. "We've got work to do back home!"

Home. Just the word made Anna smile. Arendelle was not just where she hung her cape . . . and boots . . . and . . . well, all her outdoor wear—it was also part of her family. It was where her people lived. It was her kingdom, and she wanted—no, she *needed*—to get every detail of the Polar Nights celebration just right. It was like she'd told Elsa: she loved being queen, but sometimes she got so wrapped up in the big stuff, the little details got overlooked. Getting away from her responsibilities for the night was supposed to be the break she needed.

But this morning, staring at the sky, Anna felt anxious again. The Polar Nights festival was the first weeklong celebration she was in charge of as queen, and there was so much to do before it started in just a few days. Not to mention Elsa's surprise birthday party on the festival's final night.

"Let's go! No need to pack up neatly," Anna told Kristoff as he sleepily wandered out of the tent. "Just throw it all in the wagon, like this!" She tossed all their cookware into the back and heard it land with a loud crash. "See? Easy!"

"My back is killing me," Kristoff groaned as Sven

emerged behind him. "And I barely slept a wink. Sven, your snoring is getting worse." Sven gave him a baleful look.

"Actually, honey, I think that was *you* snoring," Anna said, her mouth twitching. The tent had been hot and sticky between the rain and all the bodies crammed in it, and no one seemed to sleep well except Kristoff, who dozed right off and then woke her up with his snoring.

"I slept great!" Olaf said, bounding out of the tent. "Sleepovers are the best, aren't they?" He looked at Sven, who seemed to be stretching out his legs. "Maybe we should have one every night! True fact! Did you know studies show people who share a room are less anxious individuals and are better at negotiating conflicts?"

"Is that so?" Anna carried their picnic basket to the wagon and tossed that in as well. "This true fact wouldn't have anything to do with the campfire story last night, would it?"

Olaf sidled up to Elsa and Anna. "I didn't want to say anything," he whispered, "but I'm worried about Sven. He can't stop talking about Sinister Sissel."

Anna made a face. "Sinister Sissel?"

"You know! The Vesterland sister who turned into an evil draugr monster!" Olaf said. "Sven is terrified."

"Sven, huh?" Elsa asked as Sven brayed moanfully. "He's still scared?"

"Yep." Olaf looked innocently from one sister to the other. "He told me he's sure Sinister Sissel is still out there, just waiting to snatch us like she tried to do last night when she tore our tent."

"Olaf, for the thousandth time, it was the storm that knocked down everything," Elsa reminded him as she watched Kristoff carry the tent poles. Sven walked carefully behind him, balancing the rest of the items on his back.

"Branches tore the tent, and . . ." Kristoff spun around. "Wait. Where was I going with these things?"

Anna grabbed the poles and practically threw them into the wagon, then dragged Kristoff to the front and motioned to the bench. "Where you're going is back to Arendelle." She was done with tales of mythical monsters. Especially when there was so much real-life work to do. "I've got to meet with Helmut about his ice sculptures, and you don't want me to be late, do you?"

"Never." Kristoff kissed her, then hitched Sven to the wagon as Anna, Elsa (with Bruni), and Olaf climbed aboard, the campsite all clear. "Let's get our queen back to her castle."

Fortunately, the ride was quick. Or maybe it just felt quick because Olaf stopped talking about the draugr when they reached the first pasture and he nodded off. Even Anna fell asleep, memories of the storm and all she still had to do for the celebrations disappearing— or at least being set aside briefly. When she awoke, the wagon was already rolling through the village. Anna sat up, pleasantly surprised to see everyone out and hard at work even though the clock tower in the square had just struck two—which was usually the time they broke for a nice late lunch.

"Your Majesty, how was your trip?" asked Mattias as he greeted the wagon and offered Anna his hand to step down. While Mattias and some of his soldiers had spent thirty-four years trapped in the Enchanted Forest, the general still looked dashing with his dark salt-and-pepper hair and beard. "Did you rest up for the week ahead?" he asked, his green Arendellian uniform's medals glinting in the sunlight.

"Anna's not really a rester," Kristoff commented, and Anna gave him a sideways look.

"I did plenty of rester-ing. I mean resting," she said, looking around at the villagers carrying tables into the square. They placed them around the statue recently erected in honor of her parents. "But clearly everyone here didn't rest. I can't believe how much you got done already!"

The harvest flag pennants that had been hanging throughout the village streets had been replaced with winter ones that were pale blue and featured snowflakes. A stage had been set up in one corner of the square, where a band was practicing the waltz she hoped to dance to with Kristoff. The smell of waffles permeated the air— the Waffle Brothers were probably testing recipes for the waffle-baking competition being held as part of the festivities. And nearby, Helmut was already chipping away at large blocks of ice that would soon be turned into ice carvings.

Over at the port, Anna could see large crates being

off-loaded from ships coming in from neighboring kingdoms. That was a relief; it meant the pirate queen must still be behaving herself. The port and all the trade they did was so important to the kingdom. A blockade by pirates would cripple them by cutting off supplies and food to Arendelle, and they needed all the food they could get for the bountiful meals planned for the events ahead.

"When our queen asks for help, Arendelle is there to answer the call," Mattias said with a smile. "Even our intrepid reporter Wael has been working overtime," he added, producing a folded newspaper from his pocket. It was a copy of the *Village Crown*, Arendelle's official newspaper. Mattias smiled at Anna. "I thought you'd like to see your first-ever interview as queen."

The group applauded, with Sven emitting a whistle. Anna blushed, taking the paper from Mattias.

"I'm not sure I gave the best interview—" she started, then frowned as her eyes caught the headline. COULD "OLD BLUE EYES" BE HEADED FOR ARENDELLE? it read, alongside a rather large sketch of the famous, fierce pirate queen snarling out at them. Anna scrunched up her face. "Um . . ."

"Oh. Sorry. That was kind of a big story. I had to bump you down a little," Wael explained. "But look under the fold!"

Anna jumped at the reporter's sudden appearance. "Where did you come from?" she asked.

"I was just over there," he answered, pointing randomly in several different directions. "Turn the paper. Your article is right there."

She sighed and flipped the paper over, then squinted at the very bottom where her interview had been moved to.

"Sorry I didn't have room for a picture," Wael apologized. "But pirates are a big story! Everyone wants to know why they're in the harbor, while the kingdom already knows why you're queen." He cleared his throat. "I mean, of course we're thrilled about it. It's just . . ."

"I'm sure the interview is wonderful," Elsa offered.

Anna looked up at her sister. "There were just so many different ways to answer the questions, and I wanted to make sure my responses were just right," she admitted.

"I did have to shorten a few of them," Wael added. "You know, for space."

Mattias jumped in, holding out his hand to Elsa. "Queen Elsa, it's so good to have you back for the week."

"It's nice to be back, General Mattias," Elsa said as a wind whipped past her, carrying the rest of the dead leaves in the streets away like a makeshift broom.

The general nodded appreciatively. "And I see you've brought a helper."

"Yup." Elsa smiled at the Wind Spirit. "Gale is along to assist with whatever you need. As I told Anna, we want to be put to work."

"Work!" Olaf repeated, stretching and hopping out of the wagon. "How can anyone work when Sinister Sissel might be lurking nearby?" He glanced worriedly up at the perfectly blue sky, holding one hand out as if testing for rain.

"Not again." Kristoff shook his head. "Sven, let's go unload the wagon, then work on our snow cone recipes." He looked at Anna. "We'll be nearby if there is anything you need help with."

"Snow cones?" Elsa asked.

"The boys are setting up a booth for the festival," Anna said proudly.

"If Sinister Sissel doesn't stop them," Olaf reminded her.

"Sinister Sissel?" Mattias questioned as Mr. Aldring,

the clockmaker, walked over to show Anna his latest creation.

"Oh, it's just a name of someone from a spooky story Kristoff told last night," Anna explained, waving a hand dismissively before stuffing the newspaper into her satchel. She'd read the article later, when she was alone. Not like it would take long. "It was about these princesses from a nearby kingdom who died tragically."

"One of them killed her sister. And then her sister came back as an evil draugr to seek revenge!" Olaf explained cheerfully.

"What's a draugr?" asked a little girl holding the hand of an even smaller boy.

"It's like a zombie that can control the weather," Olaf offered. He hopped up on the nearest table to get a better view of the people walking over to listen in on the conversation. "With claws and fangs and really bad breath. It showed up at our campfire last night and caused a terrible storm, then tore our tent to shreds!"

"*Olaf!*" Anna glanced at the children, who had started clutching each other's hands a bit tighter.

"A draugr tore your tent?" gasped Gretchen, a painter, her paintbrush still between her fingers and dripping green paint onto the cobblestones. She'd been tasked with making a banner welcoming visitors to the Polar Nights festivities. So far, she'd used all the colors found in the aurora borealis.

"No," Anna insisted. "A *storm* tore our tent. As for Inger and Sissel, that was just a story."

"Yeah, and if you tell a draugr's story on the night they died? They come after you!" Olaf reiterated with a shiver. "Kristoff said so!"

"It's true," Gretchen agreed. "My mother always said, 'Don't tell tall tales about draugrs or they'll haunt you.'"

Olaf nodded knowingly.

"Hold on a second," Mattias said. "Did you say Inger and Sissel? You mean the Vesterland sisters? That's who you're talking about?"

"You've heard of them?" Anna couldn't help being intrigued.

"You haven't?" asked Mr. Aldring, scratching his head. "Well, I guess I haven't heard anyone talk about them for years. But it was a huge story when it happened. They were visiting Arendelle when Inger killed Sissel."

"I heard Inger was jealous of her sister's crown," Tuva

the blacksmith said, approaching with two iron lanterns that she placed on one of the tables.

"Sibling jealousy," her wife, Ada, agreed. She had an identical pair of lanterns in her hands. "I heard Inger was spoiled and cruel and wanted to be queen."

"I remember this! My mother used to tell us this story when my sister and I were fighting," Gretchen exclaimed excitedly. "She'd say, 'You don't want to wind up like the Vesterland sisters, do you?'"

"Yes, but what exactly happened?" Elsa pressed.

"What happened is Sissel the princess became Sissel the draugr!" Olaf said, and turned to the others. "At least according to Kristoff. And he would never lie about something so important!"

"It was only a story!" Anna cried, exasperated. She realized more people were drawing closer, intrigued. She turned to Olaf. "I mean, the draugr part, anyway. It's just something Kristoff made up."

"Though, to be fair, Sissel *could* have turned into a draugr," mused Edgar, one of the wood crafters. "After all, from what I heard, her body was never found. And she definitely had a good reason to rise from the dead and seek revenge."

"True," Gretchen agreed. "I mean, after what her evil sister did to her!"

"Should we be talking about this so close to the anniversary?" Mr. Aldring said, sounding anxious as he looked around. "We don't want to anger a draugr and make it appear."

The crowd broke out into nervous murmurs. A young boy shivered. Olaf put an arm around him. "Don't worry. I'm *sure* the dark creature with the sharp claws didn't decide to follow us home to Arendelle to finish the job it started."

The boy burst into tears.

Anna groaned. "Not helping, Olaf," she muttered, yanking the snowman away from the youngster. Then she jumped up on a nearby table, clapping her hands to get the townsfolk's attention. The wind was starting to pick up again, making the flags blow in the breeze. Great. She hoped they weren't in for another storm.

"Okay, everyone," she said. "Enough about silly mythical draugrs and dead princesses. Let's get back to work. We have a celebration to plan!"

But no one was listening. And no one was working. Instead, they couldn't stop talking about Olaf's monster and the two Vesterland princesses. It seemed every person had something to add to the story: "Inger had tried to kill her sister twice before with poison fruit!" "Every time Sissel got a new doll, Inger would cut off its head!" Some had a different take on draugrs.

"I heard they make chocolate moldy!" claimed Mrs. Blodget.

"I heard they like to steal slippers," added Mr. Aldring. "And cheese!"

Olaf frowned. "Now that you mention it, I haven't seen my slippers recently. . . ."

"You don't wear slippers," Elsa reminded him. Anna watched as her sister glanced up at the sky. The clouds were rolling in faster now. Something was definitely on the way. "Also," Elsa added, "even if draugrs existed, that doesn't mean there was one at our campfire last night. Gale and I searched the place thoroughly. I'm pretty sure if there was an evil monster lurking nearby, we would have seen it."

"Maybe it was invisible!" exclaimed Helmut. "I heard draugrs can turn invisible under the full moon!"

"I heard draugrs can turn other people into draugrs by

sneezing on them," added a fisherman who was coming up from the docks with a basketful of trout.

Behind him, a woman carrying flowers stepped out of her shop and sneezed. Everyone turned to look at her, horrified.

"Allergies!" she protested.

Anna groaned. This was getting out of hand. "Look, everyone . . ." she started.

But the words died in her throat as the sky suddenly grew black as night, as if someone had snuffed out a candle. Then the wind whipped up, blowing trees sideways. Everyone looked around in confusion. Their faces filled with fear.

"It's Sinister Sissel!" Olaf cried in alarm. "She's followed us home, and now she's going to destroy Arendelle!"

CHAPTER FIVE

Elsa

ELSA WATCHED AS EVERYONE screamed and began to scatter, diving into random buildings or running to their homes. Soon the entire village was empty, with only Anna, Kristoff, Olaf, Sven, Mattias, and Elsa herself remaining.

Anna scowled as she looked around the deserted square. A flyer for the Polar Nights festival blew by her feet. With a groan, she bent down and plucked it from the ground as it swirled around. "Olaf, you scared everyone away."

"Huh." Olaf looked around, surprised. "I do have that effect on people sometimes."

Anna balled up the flyer in her hands. "Ugh. This is getting ridiculous. There is no dangerous draugr!" she called out to the empty square. "It's just a story! And this is just another storm."

"Is it, though?" Mattias looked at the sky, scrunching up his eyebrows in worry. "I mean, even with the Polar Nights coming, this is awfully dark for midday."

Elsa's eyes rose to the sky, trepidation flickering through her. The darkness was strange. There was also something about the air. Dry, stale, with a hint of electricity crackling beneath the surface. "Mattias is right. This can't be the Polar Nights," she mused. "They bring about a beautiful blue twilight hue. This sky is much gloomier and darker. Like the kind of darkness you get just before a big rainstorm."

"Then where is the rain? Or the thunder?" Kristoff asked pointedly. The sky was so dark now that it was hard to see him even though he was just a few feet away. "It's windy, yes, but otherwise the sky just looks strangely black."

Elsa nodded, her unease intensifying. It was almost as if a heavy blanket had been thrown over the sun. In all her years in Arendelle, she'd never seen anything like it. She pursed her lips. "Bruni," she said slowly. "Go ahead and light the streetlamps, won't you?"

The Fire Spirit leapt up, happy to be given a task. It scrambled up a lamppost, lit the lamp, and scurried down again to head to the next. Elsa followed right behind, waving her hands and casting icy mirrors under the lampposts. The ice reflected the fire and brightened the square. Soon it felt like daylight again.

"Okay," Anna called, "you can all come out now!" She ran to the butcher's door and banged on it. Then she ran to the baker's. "It's fine. Everything's fine! No draugr! Just some freakish weather! No murderous monsters in sight!"

"What about *out* of sight?" Olaf asked, glancing fearfully at a dark corner between two buildings. Anna shot him a look as Kristoff grabbed him by the branch and dragged him toward Blodget's Bakery, where a few folks were emerging sheepishly, clearly realizing their queen was a lot braver than they were.

"Come on, Olaf," Kristoff said. "Let's get some chocolate. I've heard chocolate is very good at protecting against monsters."

"Is it?" Olaf's eyes brightened. "What a great fun fact!" Kristoff gave him one final yank and they disappeared into the shop, the door banging shut behind them.

Elsa snorted, then turned back to the town square, where more people emerged warily from their homes and shops and gathered in small groups around the statue honoring Iduna and Agnarr. They still looked uneasy and kept glancing worriedly up at the sky. Elsa knew those looks all too well. It was exactly how they'd reacted when she accidentally woke the spirits of the Enchanted Forest.

Could this be some kind of magical event as well?

Anna leapt up on the makeshift stage that had been abandoned by the band. Pushing aside a harp, she clapped her hands to get the people's attention.

"Look," she said. "I know this weather is strange, but there has to be a logical explanation. A weather anomaly. Those definitely happen. Especially this time of year."

"What if it's the draugr?" called out a little boy. He plugged a grubby thumb in his mouth and looked up at his mother with concern. "What if it's after us all?"

"One, there is no such thing as draugrs," Anna declared. "And two, even if there were, we have the best soldiers in the land. General Mattias would never let some silly monster invade Arendelle. Would you, Mattias?"

"Of course not, Your Majesty," he declared, standing tall and proud. "We will strengthen our patrols tonight, just in case. But I'm sure there's nothing to worry about."

"Except our Polar Nights celebration!" Anna added, a little too enthusiastically. She was wearing a bit of a frenzied smile on her face. "Which isn't going to plan itself! So . . . uh, everyone back to work so we can break early and have an ice cream party in the castle this afternoon!"

The crowd cheered and began to disperse, going back to what they'd been doing before the strange weather event commenced. Elsa could still hear a few of them muttering about the darkness—and the draugr—while a few were even still discussing Sissel and Inger. But hey, at least they weren't cowering in fear anymore. Thank goodness her sister was such a capable leader. That could have gone much worse.

Anna leapt off the stage and headed over to her. "I told them there was nothing to worry about," she said loudly, smiling at a few of the townspeople across the way. Then her voice lowered to a whisper—for Elsa's ears only. "But what if there is? I mean, this weather does seem really unusual, don't you think?"

Elsa nodded absently. She stared up again at the dark sky. Had it gotten a little brighter? No, it was still really dark. "I think I should go talk to Sorenson," she said, referring to the Arendellian scientist who lived some distance from town. He had been helpful the last time Arendelle had fallen under a curse. "He might have some answers."

"Good idea," Anna agreed. "I'll go saddle up Havski." The swift stallion had been her horse since childhood. "It's a few hours' ride, but if we leave now, we can be back by . . ." She stopped, glancing up at the sky. "Well, maybe not dark . . ."

Elsa shook her head. "Anna, you should stay here. Keep getting ready for the Polar Nights festivities. You said yourself that there's a lot to do."

"It can wait," Anna declared, placing her hands on her hips. "I mean, the festival is important, yes. But so are you. And I'm not about to let you go wandering off on your own when there could be a monster on the loose."

"Oh, so now you believe in the draugr?" Elsa raised an eyebrow. She knew she could argue with her sister about this. But she also knew she wouldn't win. And deep down, she realized she preferred to have Anna by her side. Their best adventures, after all, had always been ones they had together. And they still had a lot of catching up to do.

"I believe in keeping my sister safe," Anna declared. "Besides, Kristoff can stay and be in charge. He's going to be a member of the royal family soon. Might as well get his feet wet."

Kristoff, who had been walking by with an armful of snow cones, stopped in his tracks. "Wait, what?"

Anna beamed at him. "You can stay here and keep everyone on task, right? While Elsa and I try to figure out what's going on?"

"Of course," Kristoff declared without the slightest pause. "Whatever you need. I'm your man." He tapped his chest proudly, accidentally dropping one of the snow cones on the ground in the process. Sven quickly slurped it up.

"Thanks, honey! You're the best!" Anna stood on her tiptoes to give him a kiss, then dashed toward the stables. Kristoff looked at Elsa, his easy smile fading a little.

"You'll keep her safe?" he asked.

"We'll keep each other safe," she told him, laying a reassuring hand on his shoulder. "Nothing will happen. I promise."

"I'm holding you to that," he said with a wag of his finger before turning to distribute his remaining cones. Elsa watched him for a moment, then turned toward the castle, figuring she'd stop by the kitchen to grab some food for the road before she called for her own steed, the Water Nokk. As she walked across the bridge, she took one last look at the dark sky. An involuntary shiver slipped down her spine.

"Surely, there's got to be a logical explanation," she told herself as she stepped into the castle. "And Sorenson will be able to make sense of it all."

"This doesn't make any sense!"

Sorenson paced the tower room, flipping his long beard over his shoulder as he stared at some astronomical charts he had hung on the walls. He picked up an old copper sundial, turning it over in his hands before setting it back down on the desk.

Elsa glanced at Anna. So much for an easy scientific explanation.

"Could it just be that the Polar Nights came early?" she asked, knowing she was grasping at straws.

"No." Sorenson shook his head. "I've mapped out the sun in its relation to the planet, and it's not due to slip below our horizon for another week. Besides, around these parts, the Polar Nights only give off a soft blue glow. Not this suffocating blackness. It's almost as if we're experiencing a solar eclipse. But there isn't one scheduled for the next twenty-five years." He raked a hand through his graying hair, shaking his head. "I don't know what to tell you. There is no scientific explanation for any of this."

Elsa sank down into a nearby chair, discouraged. It hadn't been easy getting here. Sorenson lived in the middle of nowhere, and navigating their way through the darkness had been a challenge even with the Water Nokk guiding her. She'd really been hoping it would at least be worth the trip.

Instead, it seemed, it was a complete dead end.

"You don't think it could be something . . . magical?" she asked hesitantly. She didn't want to mention the silly draugr theory, but could there be something else out there causing this?

Sorenson shook his head. "I'm a scientist," he reminded them. "I deal in facts and logic. If it's magical answers you seek, you need to check with the trolls. That's more their thing."

Anna frowned. "The trolls are really busy this time of year with their crystal celebration. I don't want to bother them unless it's really necessary."

"You might not have a choice," Sorensen said grimly. "Sometimes things are out of the realm of science, and while it pains me to admit it, this is not the first time I've seen this sort of strange change in the weather." He pulled at his beard. "The last time it happened, I was just a boy, but I remember everyone saying it was the work of a draugr."

Elsa and Anna looked at each other.

"Wait, you believe in draugrs?" Anna asked. "But you're a scientist!"

"I know, but I remember my father being certain he

saw a draugr once—and my father was not a man easily fooled," Sorenson said, leaning against a long table for support. "He talked about that draugr and its relation to the weather with such detail that I found myself believing him."

Elsa couldn't suppress a shudder. If Sorenson believed in draugrs, maybe they should be concerned.

Sorenson shrugged. "But then again, I didn't see the creature myself. In any case, it might be something you want to mention to the trolls."

Anna side-eyed Elsa nervously. "We will bring it up to them. Thank you, Sorenson."

Elsa rose to her feet. "Let's go back to Arendelle," she said. "We'll check on everyone first. Then we'll figure out the next steps—if that's even necessary." She shrugged. "Who knows? Maybe the sun will rise tomorrow and everything will be back to normal."

The two sisters said their goodbyes to Sorenson and headed home by horseback, the Water Nokk once again leading the way. But even the water horse's icy glow seemed a little dimmer as they pushed through the marsh. The blackness hovered over them as if it were a living thing.

"This is getting really creepy," Anna remarked, reaching up to push away a low-hanging branch from a nearby tree. "Especially after Sorenson brought up the draugr thing, too. I mean, that man only believes in facts. Could Kristoff's story really have summoned Sinister Sissel?"

"Oh, don't start with that nickname again." Elsa choked out a laugh, but it no longer felt very funny. "Even if there *is* a draugr out there, that doesn't mean it's the reanimated corpse of some random princess who died years ago."

"But it *could* be," Anna argued. "And to be honest, I wouldn't blame the girl one bit! I mean, being murdered by your own sister in cold blood? I might decide to come back as an unhinged evil monster ready to seek revenge, too!"

Elsa couldn't help cringing a little after Anna spoke. Suddenly she wasn't thinking of the Vesterland sisters anymore, but of seeing her own sister, Anna, ice cold on the ballroom floor when they were children. And herself, screaming desperately for their parents. If anything had happened to her sister that night . . .

Anna's face turned ashen in the darkness. "Oh my gosh! I'm so sorry. I didn't mean . . ." She clamped a hand over her mouth. "I'll just shut up now."

"No. It's okay," Elsa assured her with a small smile. "I know that you know I'd never hurt you on purpose."

"Of course not," Anna affirmed. "The whole thing was just an accident, pure and simple. I know that for a fact, even if I don't remember it happening."

Elsa cringed again. Anna had never recovered the memories the trolls had taken from her the night of the accident. So many memories of them growing up together, lost forever.

Which meant it was up to Elsa to keep them alive.

She paused for a moment, thinking. "I know we don't talk about what happened when we were kids very much. And I get it—I really do. But if you ever wanted to . . . well, I wouldn't mind, you know."

Anna's eyes widened. "Really?"

"It's good to look back sometimes," Elsa assured her. "At all our memories—even the bad ones. I've been doing that a lot in Ahtohallan, and it's actually helped me get over some things. And I'd love to share some of them with you. . . ." She stroked the Water Nokk's mane thoughtfully, feeling its icy waves ripple through her fingers. "Our whole childhood was filled with secrets. Our parents', mine . . ." She cocked her head. "Did *you* have any secrets?"

"Wouldn't you like to know!" Anna grinned mischievously. Elsa laughed.

"Okay, fine." Elsa mock-pouted. "In any case, I'm glad we've put all that behind us and we can talk openly."

"Me too!" Anna declared. Then she sighed.

"What's wrong?" Elsa asked, concerned by her sister's expression.

"It's just . . ." Anna shrugged. "I don't know. Nothing, I guess."

"No secrets, remember?"

"Okay, right. It's just that . . . sometimes I can't help but be sad about all the time we lost together when we were growing up," Anna noted. "I don't mean just the missing memories. But all those years we spent apart. I should have tried harder to talk to you. . . ."

Elsa shuddered, remembering that terrible time when

she'd locked herself in her room. How lonely she'd been. How desperate and sad.

"I regret that, too," she said softly. "I could have really used a sister back then. But instead, I pushed you away. I was just so scared of hurting you again. And yet, in the end, I did hurt you. Just in a different way."

"It wasn't your fault," Anna insisted. "You were just a kid. And you were scared. I don't blame you for any of it. I'm just glad you're all right now. That you're not afraid of your powers anymore. And that they've become an important part of who you are. You're the Snow Queen. You're powerful. Magical." She smiled warmly. "And yet, at the end of the day, you'll always be my sister."

Elsa's heart clenched when she gazed at her sister's face. She hadn't always deserved Anna's love. But she was so grateful to have it. "And you'll always be mine . . . Queen of Arendelle."

Anna blushed hard. "I still get weirded out by that title sometimes."

"Well, you've more than earned it," Elsa assured her. She met her sister's eyes with her own. "In any case, we can't change the past," she added. "All we can do is keep moving forward. And make new memories, together."

Anna grinned. "Sounds good to—"

Her words were cut off by a sudden wailing sound.

"What was that?" Elsa whispered, slowing the Water Nokk. The spirit pricked its ears. Clearly it had heard it, too. "Wolves?"

Anna shook her head, looking just as confused—and scared—as Elsa felt. "That didn't sound like wolves."

"No," Elsa agreed, feeling the hairs on the back of her neck stand on end. "It sounded like . . ." She trailed off. What *did* it sound like? Like nothing she'd ever heard before. She squinted into the darkness, urging the spirit onward.

ARRR!!!

The Water Nokk reared backward, icy water spraying from its mane and soaking Elsa's dress as something leapt out of the bushes. Or was it someone? Elsa couldn't take her eyes off it, heart pounding in her chest. It was clearly human-shaped, but that was where all similarities ended. It had blackened skin, misshapen bones that jutted out at weird angles, and green slime oozing from its pores. Elsa shuddered as the thing seemed to grin madly at them. Its teeth were broken, darkened, and dripping with something suspiciously red.

"Oh my gosh," Anna whispered. "Is that . . . is that . . . ?"

"The draugr!" Elsa cried in horror. "It's real!"

CHAPTER SIX

Anna

ANNA FROZE.

Had Elsa just said *draugr*? As she stared at the ghastly creature slowly gliding toward them, Anna knew there was no other explanation. Olaf and Kristoff had been right.

The draugr looked from Elsa to Anna, reaching out for them with blackened hands and sharp nails, gnashing what was left of its rotting teeth. Anna jumped, her heartbeat quickening as the draugr hissed. It sounded like a snake. Then it let out the eeriest of moans. The sound went right through her.

Thunder rumbled in the distance and Anna felt the

wind pick up, making some of the trees around them sway violently. She glanced at the sky; it was just as dark as it had been before in the village, but this time a storm was moving in fast.

"Anna, we need to go now! Follow me!" Elsa cried as the Water Nokk instantly reacted, racing out of the draugr's reach.

"On it! Havski, let's move!" Anna turned to follow the Water Spirit's icy path when *CRACK!*

Lightning struck a massive tree in front of her, sending it crashing to the ground. Anna pulled on Havski's reins just in time to keep them from being hit. The trunk hit the ground with a quake. Startled, Havski reared on his back legs.

"Easy!" Anna cried out, reaching for the reins again to calm the horse. But she was too late. Anna flew off his back, landing hard on the ground, her head smacking against what felt like a rock. Pain seared through her body and the world lost focus for a second, but Anna fought her way back, sitting up in time to see Havski bolt in the opposite direction.

"Anna! Where are you!" Elsa cried out from somewhere on the other side of the downed tree.

"Here! I'm all right!" Anna lied. Her hands flew to her head and she winced as she felt something wet. Sticky. Was she bleeding? Was it bad? How was she getting out of there? The downed tree seemed to have hit two more as it dropped, and they had fallen like huge dominos, forming a giant barricade so tall and wide Anna couldn't even see her sister through it. It was amazing she hadn't been killed. "But I don't know how I'm getting around this."

"We'll get to you!" Elsa said, her voice sounding strained. "Just keep away from the draugr!"

Anna's eyes shot open. *Draugr.* How had she forgotten about the draugr? She whipped her head around just in time to see the creature stalking toward her, red slime dripping from its grotesque mouth. She had to get out of there!

"*Sissssstterrrrrrr. . . .*"

Anna froze. What was that? Was that the draugr? Had it just said *sister*? A chill tripped down her spine.

"*Sissssstterrrrrrr. . . .*"

The draugr could talk! "Sister? No, thank you! I've already got one." She couldn't wait for Elsa and the Water Nokk to reach her. Her head was pounding so hard she wasn't sure she could stand.

"Myyyyyy sissssssttttterrrrr," the draugr hissed, dragging what was left of its wretched body in tattered clothing toward her.

Thump. Drag.

Thump. Drag.

Thump. Drag.

Run! Anna told herself, pushing her body to stand even as her vision blurred. She tried to step forward, but her left leg wouldn't budge. She looked down in surprise. Her foot was caught in between several thick, winding roots. She must have gotten ensnared when she fell. Anna tugged on her leg—hard—but it was stuck, seemingly fastened in place.

The draugr lunged forward again, and Anna winced as it reached out with blackened hands. *This is it*, she thought, holding her breath, and then exhaling fast when nothing happened. She looked up in surprise. The draugr was holding her folded copy of the *Village Crown*. It must have fallen from her satchel when she had been thrown from Havski. The draugr looked from Anna to the paper and back at Anna again. What was left of its face curled into a snarl.

Could the draugr read? Anna suddenly thought of

Wael's story about how Anna, the younger sister, had replaced the queen on the throne.

Oh, no.

"Sissel?" Anna whispered.

The creature's face was even more grotesque than before. *"Sissssterrrrr!"* It lunged straight toward her.

Anna thought fast.

The draugr is Sissel.

Its sister tried to take its crown.

I took the crown from Elsa.

Oh, no . . .

"You don't understand," Anna begged, trying to pull her leg free once again. "Elsa gave me the crown!"

But the draugr wasn't listening. It kept coming, moaning even louder.

Thump. Drag.

It was almost on top of her now. Panic gripped Anna as she tried to yank her foot free in desperation. Her boot was completely wedged. "Come on, come on, come on," Anna begged, willing her foot to miraculously loosen somehow, trying to wiggle her toes, her ankle, grip her boot harder—anything—to pull herself free. But it was no use. The draugr was bearing down on her. Elsa wasn't going to make it to her in time. The thing was so close, Anna could smell the rot coming off it, making her want to vomit. Her mind suddenly went to the villagers' talk of draugrs. If this thing sneezed on her, would she turn into a draugr?

Anna spun around, looking for something to defend herself with. Her eyes landed on a bare branch from the tree she was tangled in. Reaching up with two hands, she snapped one of the largest twigs off clean. She whirled around, brandishing it like a sword.

"Stay back!" Anna commanded. "Back!"

For a moment, the draugr seemed confused; its creepy smile disappeared.

"That's right! I'm in charge here!" Anna said, feeling slight relief. She was the boss! Not this icky, crawly thing that had slipped through the darkened day trying to terrify her and her horse. A flash of lightning lit up the midnight path. "Stay away from me and my sister!"

The draugr's hollowed eyes widened and its smile returned, appearing even more gruesome than it had before. Anna cringed as a worm slid its way out of the draugr's mouth.

"*Sisssttttterrrrrrrr!*" it moaned again.

"No!" Anna shouted. "I won't let you hurt us!" Anna swatted the air in front of the creature with her branch, trying to scare it.

The creature roared, pushing forward again, bearing down on Anna now. She leaned back, and that was when she heard it—*whoosh!*

Ice cracked across the ground, forming a sheet beneath Anna and the draugr's feet.

Whoosh! Elsa and the Water Nokk had made it around the barricade and were running her way. Elsa shot sheet after sheet of ice at the draugr.

The ice formed around Anna's feet and more importantly around the roots Anna's boot was caught in. She watched as it crackled, freezing in place over the vines and branches. Maybe now she could crack the roots, brittle from the ice on them, and free herself. She whacked at them with the branch and heard a snap. Anna yanked on her foot again and felt herself freefalling backward. Unable to right herself in time, she landed on her behind.

Angered, the draugr shot forward toward Anna yet again. Anna scurried back on her hands and feet, racing to get out of its way.

Whoosh! More ice appeared, forming a barrier between them that lasted but a moment. Seconds later, the draugr broke through it with its nails.

"*Sisterrrrrrrrrrrr,*" it moaned. "*Myyyyyyyyy!*"

The Water Nokk skidded to a stop by Anna's side, and Elsa reached down with a free hand and yanked Anna up off the ground, helping her stand. But the draugr kept coming at them even as Elsa wielded more ice and snow in an attempt to form a huge wall between them. For a moment, it was working, but then to Anna's surprise, her sister's ice-forming capabilities seemed to sputter out, coming in drips rather than spurts, like a well running dry.

"It isn't working!" Anna cried, holding her head, which was still throbbing.

"I know!" Elsa said, looking anguished as she tried again and again to make sheets of solid ice. But only small shots of ice appeared. The ice wall thickened, but not enough to keep the draugr at bay. "Something's wrong!"

"We have to get out of here, but Havski took off!" Anna said as the wind started moaning, its sounds matching the draugr's as the creature pushed its way against the ice separating them, trying to clear a path to reach them.

"You're riding with me!" ordered Elsa as she reached for Anna's hand to pull her up on the Water Nokk.

Anna stepped forward and, *whoa*—stumbled. She felt her knees buckle. The world spun around her. Black spots appeared before her eyes.

"Anna!" Elsa cried, jumping off the horse and grabbing her sister.

"I'm okay, I just feel dizzy, and my ankle isn't helping much, either," Anna admitted.

Elsa touched Anna's head, seeing the blood on her fingertips. "You can't ride like this. It isn't safe."

Crack! Anna watched as the draugr's razor-sharp nails sliced through the protective sheet of ice, sending snow flying everywhere. The wall was coming down. They were running out of time.

"*Sissttteerrrrrrr!*" it moaned again, trying desperately to reach them.

Elsa leapt in front of Anna, facing off with the draugr. She stared down the creature, a fierce look on her face, as if daring it to come closer.

"Elsa! No!" Anna cried.

The draugr lunged forward, grabbing Elsa's hand with its twisted claws. Anna watched in horror as her sister tried to jerk her hand away, but the creature seemed too strong. For a moment, they just stared at each other. Then Elsa's eyes began to soften. A strange expression began to come over her face. Like she was going into a trance.

"Elsa!" Anna tried again.

Elsa seemed to come back at the sound of Anna's voice. She jerked her hand away, and this time she was successful at breaking free. The draugr screeched in rage and tried to grab her again, but the Water Nokk charged at the creature, blocking its path.

Elsa turned to Anna, her face frantic. "We need to find someplace to hide. Let's go that way!" She pointed to a break in the trees behind them and a narrow path that looked like it could be navigated—even in the dark. "The Water Nokk will hold it off."

The draugr let out a loud moan that made the hair on Anna's arms stand on end. She watched as the water horse faced off with the creature, whinnying fiercely. Drawing in a breath, Anna tried to stumble forward, with Elsa guiding her. But after only a few steps, the world spun again and her ankle gave out. The two sisters toppled over each other and onto the ground. Anna looked up at Elsa, her body trembling. "I'm sorry! I can't—"

Suddenly, she realized Elsa's eyes were no longer on her, but staring behind her. Fear gripped her heart. "It's right behind us, isn't it?" she croaked.

"Actually . . ." Elsa shook her head in disbelief. "Actually, it's not."

"Wait, what?" Anna whipped her head around, fully expecting to come face to face with a monster. But no . . . Elsa was right. Her mouth dropped open in shock. There was nothing there.

The draugr had completely disappeared.

CHAPTER SEVEN

Elsa

"COME ON, ANNA. Just a few more steps."

Elsa helped her sister to the entrance of the little hut and used her foot to kick open the door. Anna stumbled inside.

"How did you find an old shepherd's hut out here?" Anna asked, looking around once she'd caught her breath.

"I caught a glimpse of it as we were walking and hoped it was still intact," Elsa replied, after lighting some of the candles around the room. "I'm just glad it's here for us to use for the night." Their parents had commissioned these structures to be erected all over Arendelle years before so shepherds could use them to shelter with their animals when the weather got bad. (Which meant that while the huts were usually dry, they also often smelled like wet sheep.)

"It seems okay. Though it doesn't look like anyone's used this one for a while," Anna noted, running a finger along a table and leaving a dusty trail. She sneezed.

"Doesn't seem like it," Elsa agreed, settling down on a stool across from her sister. When she'd realized how bad Anna's ankle was, not to mention her throbbing head, she knew better than to try to get her on the Water Nokk and whisk her back to Arendelle. Anna needed time to rest and recover before making a long journey on horseback. "At least it's dry," Elsa added. A drip of water from the roof then landed on her shoulder. She frowned. "Well, semidry anyway."

"It's perfect. And so are you," Anna said, reaching up to rub her head as she settled onto her own stool.

"Are you okay?" Elsa asked worriedly, noting the blood crusting in her sister's hair. How hard, she wondered, had Anna hit her head on that rock?

Anna nodded, pulling her hand away. "It probably looks much worse than it is," she assured her. "I hardly feel it anymore." She reached down to her ankle. "This, on the other hand . . ." She grimaced. "I can't believe I got stuck in a tree and wrapped around a stupid root while a draugr was coming after us! That thing would have killed me if you hadn't come back."

"It could have killed both of us," Elsa mused, half to herself. "But instead, it just disappeared. Where do you think it went?"

"I don't know," Anna said with a frown. "Maybe it only has limited magic? And it ran out or something and had to go and recharge?"

"Maybe . . ." Elsa shook her head, mystified. "We definitely need to find out more about these creatures. So we'll know what to do if we run into one again." She gave a half smile. "Not that you didn't make a great stand against it. You were so brave, yelling at it like that! It was like you weren't even scared at all."

Elsa thought back to the scene. Speaking of scared, for a moment, when the trees had come down between them, she'd been terrified she wouldn't be able to rescue her sister. That after all they'd been through, this . . . horrible creature . . . would be the end of Anna (or the both of them). She shuddered. It was too awful of a thought to dwell on.

"Please. I'm not about to let Sinister Sissel get the best of me!" Anna declared, puffing out her chest.

"So you really think it was Sissel?" Elsa asked, scratching her head. "That Kristoff's story has come to life?" It seemed so impossible to her, even after all they had just witnessed.

"I know it sounds crazy, but look at the facts," Anna replied, her tone and look ultraserious. "You heard Sorenson—draugrs can control the weather, and the minute Kristoff told that story, boom! We have scary dark skies, violent storms . . . now a monster come to life. I mean, I'm putting two and two together, and I'm not getting five."

Elsa glanced at the storm outside. It had picked up again, the rain battering at the windows. Another drop landed on her forehead. "Maybe you're right. Kristoff did say if you told a draugr's story, you could bring it back. . . ."

Anna swallowed hard. "There's something more. When I fell, my satchel spilled open with the copy of my article in the *Village Crown*. You know, the one where Wael interviewed me about taking your place as queen?" Her frown deepened. "The creature picked it up and started freaking out. Like the article upset it or something."

"Why?" Elsa shot her a puzzled look. "What would a draugr care about a newspaper? Can they even read?"

"If they were once human, maybe. And I mean, think about it!" Anna exclaimed. "I'm the younger sister! I'm just like Inger! And I have the crown. Sissel probably thinks I stole it from you—just like Inger tried to steal it from her! And now she's trying to get her revenge on me, since Inger's long gone!"

Elsa raised an eyebrow. "Okay, that's a bit of a stretch."

"And yet a story-time monster literally attacking us in real life in the woods and controlling the weather isn't?" Anna answered. Her whole body was trembling now. Elsa put a comforting hand on her shoulder.

"Anna, you're upsetting yourself," she scolded gently. "It's not going to help. Whatever is going on, we'll figure it out. But I promise you, I'm not going to let some draugr get you, okay? No matter what."

"I need to get back to Arendelle," Anna declared, trying to rise to her feet. "Kristoff is there. If the draugr knows he's the one who told its story on the anniversary, it could be after him, and everyone in Arendelle. We need to warn people they could be in danger!" She winced in pain as she put weight on her ankle.

"You're not going anywhere," Elsa told her sternly. "Not on that ankle. And not in this storm."

"But Arendelle—"

"Can take care of itself. You left Kristoff and Mattias in charge. They can deal with one little monster."

Anna raised an eyebrow. "You call that little?"

"You know what I mean," Elsa chided. "I promise, the second the storm stops, I'll go out and look for Havski. Or find someone with a wagon. But right now, we both need to stay put."

Anna nodded glumly, not looking happy about the prospect of staying put. Elsa felt a pang of guilt. Maybe she should have protested harder when Anna said she wanted to come along. Of course, at the time, she hadn't known there was an actual monster in the woods. Another wave of unease seemed to waft through her stomach. Her magic had been almost useless against that thing. And at the end, it had all but sputtered out. She knew her magic wasn't limitless—no magic was, according to the Northuldra. But if it wasn't even enough to save her sister, what were they going to do if the draugr did attack the kingdom?

"Ugh. I hate feeling so useless," Anna said, glaring down at her hurt ankle.

Elsa knew exactly how she felt. "At least we got our sister time!" she said, trying to cheer her up. "And this time no one can interrupt us!"

Anna made a face. "Yeah, except for our friendly neighborhood draugr . . ."

Elsa rose to her feet and wandered over to the window. She peered outside. The storm was still raging, but fortunately there was no creature in sight. She walked over to the door and bolted it, just in case.

"The draugr—if that's what it really was—is gone," Elsa said. "And we're safe here in the hut for now." She dug into her pack. "And look!" Elsa pulled out a bag.

Anna's eyes widened. "Marshmallows? You brought marshmallows?"

Elsa shrugged. "Well, we never got a chance to roast them over our campfire. So I thought I'd bring them along. . . ." She let out a call and suddenly Bruni appeared, pushing its way through a crack in the front door, slurping the air with its tongue. Elsa led it over to the small stone hearth in the kitchen area of the hut and instructed the Fire Spirit to do its thing. A moment later there was a small blaze that gave off a warm glow.

"Oh my gosh. Best. Sister. Ever!" Anna exclaimed, her upset demeanor pushed aside. She pulled her stool closer to the fire. Elsa handed her a cooking skewer from the side of the fireplace, and Anna stabbed the marshmallow with it, holding it over the small flame. Elsa followed with her own, and soon they had two gooey golden brown marshmallows at the ends of their sticks.

"Sorry we don't have any chocolate," Elsa apologized.

"Oh, but we do!" Anna exclaimed, reaching into her own pack. She pulled out a wrapped square of paper. Elsa laughed as her sister revealed the dark-brown treasure inside. "A queen has to be prepared for all kinds of emergencies," she joked, breaking the bar in two and handing the larger piece to her sister.

"Definitely!" Elsa agreed, watching Anna pull her marshmallow from the fire and set the chocolate on top of it. Elsa did the same, breathing in the warm scent as the chocolate melted on her marshmallow. She looked up at her sister.

"Mmm. Chocolate," they said in sync. Then they giggled.

"Okay, you're making me feel a little better," Anna admitted after savoring her treat. "I'm hardly thinking at all about the monster lurking in the woods." She glanced out the window. "Hardly . . ."

Elsa sighed. She was pretty sure neither one of them was going to sleep a wink tonight. But maybe that was for the best. They didn't know when, or if, the draugr would be back. And Elsa didn't want it to catch them off guard again. Especially if her powers were really drained.

"Oops!" Anna squeaked as her second marshmallow caught fire. She yanked it out of the hearth. Elsa instinctively lifted a finger and flung a small blast of ice in the marshmallow's direction, easily quenching the flame.

Anna shot her an appreciative look. "Thanks," she said.

Elsa smiled, feeling better knowing her powers had returned—at least enough for a marshmallow emergency. It was funny; once upon a time, all she'd wanted was to rid herself of her powers. But now, even the thought of losing them terrified her. As Anna had said, they were a part of her now, for better or worse. Not a curse, like she'd once believed. But a gift that could help people. One that could literally save lives. Make the world a better place. The spirits had trusted her with this gift, and now she wanted nothing more than to prove worthy of that trust.

A thought suddenly struck Elsa. "I may have another way to distract you," she told her sister.

"Yeah?" Anna queried, looking up. Her mouth was covered in sticky white fluff. "How's that?"

"I can try the memory thing again. Like I was trying to do in the tent last night."

"I'd love that!" Anna said encouragingly. "Do you have one of Mother and Father? Maybe one of them when they were growing up?"

"I think so," Elsa said, closing her eyes for a moment to try to draw up something for her sister. Then she opened her eyes again and smiled. "Yes! I've got just the memory! I pulled it up in Ahtohallan the other day. Mother and Father were in a ballroom. Spinning around to this ridiculous dance they made up. I think they called it 'The Reindeer Who Has to Pee Really Badly but Is Stuck in a Ballroom.'"

Anna raised an eyebrow. "That sounds like quite the dance."

"I know, right? It's crazy how silly they used to be. They were so cute together. I sometimes spend hours pulling up their memories."

"You are so lucky," Anna said with a sigh. "I wish I could see it all, too."

Elsa felt a small twinge of guilt at the wistfulness she heard in her sister's voice. It wasn't fair that Anna should be locked out of these memories—after all, Iduna and Agnarr were her parents, too. But Elsa was the only one who could access Ahtohallan and its treasure trove of memories. Which meant she was going to have to get creative.

"Well, that's why I'm working on this," Elsa said. "My goal is to learn how to re-create the memories I see in Ahtohallan and bring them home to you. So you don't have to miss out on anything."

"Did I ever mention you're amazing?" Anna asked. "Because you are. Amazing."

Elsa felt her cheeks heat at the praise from her sister. Anna had always loved her magic, even when they were children, and hearing the excitement in her voice now took Elsa back to that innocent time.

Do the magic! Anna would beg, and Elsa could never deny her.

She drew in a deep breath, trying to channel the power inside of her. Then she lifted her index finger, pointing it toward the little puddle of water from the leak in the roof. She'd learned it was easier to pull things from water, because as Olaf liked to remind them, water had memory. As she closed her eyes, she tried to picture the flowing image of her parents in her mind as she'd seen them in Ahtohallan. In the ballroom. In each other's arms. Twirling and laughing and—

Suddenly her mind went blank. Completely blank— as if someone had smothered a candle. The memory she'd had in her head ceased entirely, and for a moment, she couldn't even remember what memory she'd been trying to conjure up to begin with. Something about their parents? Was that right?

Her eyes opened. She glanced apologetically at her sister. "Argh. I had it. For a second . . ." She sighed. "I'm sorry. Maybe it isn't the best night for this."

"The best night for what?" Anna asked through a

mouthful of burnt marshmallow. She waved her hand in front of her face. "I know I should wait for them to cool down, but they're just so yummy. I burn the roof of my mouth every time!"

Elsa frowned, confused. Was Anna trying to make her feel better by ignoring what had just happened? That didn't seem like something her sister would do. She'd at least ask if Elsa was okay. Wouldn't she? Instead, she was acting like nothing had happened at all.

Or as if she'd forgotten it altogether.

The same way Elsa had forgotten the memory she was trying to pull.

Concern churned in Elsa's gut. Something was wrong here. Something was very wrong. She thought back to how Anna and Kristoff had acted at the campsite last night. They'd been strangely forgetful then, too. Was it all related? Could it have something to do with the monster?

Only Ahtohallan knows . . . Her mother's voice seemed to whisper in her ears.

She drew in a breath. "Look, Anna, here's what I'm thinking. Tomorrow we'll get you back to Arendelle to make sure everyone's okay. And you can do some research on draugrs in our parents' library. Find out everything you can about the monster. Meanwhile, I'll go back to Ahtohallan and see what I can learn there. Maybe the white river can tell me something useful."

Anna swallowed her marshmallow. "Good idea," she said. "And then we'll meet back in Arendelle and compare notes. Together, I'm sure we can figure out what this draugr is doing here."

Elsa smiled at the confidence she heard in her sister's voice. Anna truly wasn't scared of anything—even when maybe she should be. Elsa admired her for that and wished she could feel the same.

But as the wind howled outside, the branches of nearby trees rapping angrily against the windowpanes, she realized she *was* afraid. For herself. For her sister.

And for Arendelle.

CHAPTER EIGHT

Anna

HORSES ARE LOYAL CREATURES, Anna thought as Elsa returned to the hut the next morning with Anna's beloved horse at her side.

"Havski!" Anna cried, hobbling toward him.

Her ankle felt much better than it had the day before, but there was no way she could have walked all the way back to Arendelle on it. If Elsa hadn't located Havski, what would she have done? She imagined her sister creating a toboggan out of ice for her or calling on the ice creature Marshmallow to leave his cozy castle at the top of the North Mountain to carry her back. Wouldn't that have been a sight—her sitting in Marshmallow's palm as she approached the village? Talk about making an entrance!

"I'm so glad Elsa found you, boy," said Anna as she moved to touch Havski's head, and he twitched. That was odd, but now that she looked at the horse closer, she realized his whole body was shaking.

"Is he okay?" Anna asked.

"I found him wandering around the pasture trying to find you," Elsa said. "He's dry, though, so he must have found shelter overnight." Elsa stroked his long black mane. "Poor guy. He must have been so scared when he saw the draugr."

"It's okay, Havski," Anna said soothingly, petting his pale gray hide. "We're safe now, and we're going home to Arendelle to . . ."

That was funny. There was something she had to do in the village, but for the life of her, she suddenly couldn't remember what it was. Anna looked at Elsa, who was watching her closely and frowning.

"To check on the people and see what you can find out about the draugr before it returns," Elsa prompted her. She placed a cool hand on her sister's cheek. "Anna, you do remember that's what we discussed last night, don't you?"

As soon as Elsa touched her, Anna felt what resembled a whooshing sensation through her brain. The memory was back! Anna was headed home to do research on draugrs in their parents' library, and Elsa was going to Ahtohallan. "Of course!" she declared with a shake of her head. Her copper-colored locks waved side to side. "Sorry! You know my brain after a bad night's sleep!"

"Speaking of night . . ." Elsa looked up at the sky, her brow creasing in worry. While they both knew it was morning, the dawn hadn't come. Instead, for the second day in a row, the world was awash in a darkness that didn't feel like night or day. There was no sun or moon in sight. The air was thick and the world quiet, as if it were just waiting for disaster to strike. Even the birds and woodland creatures seemed to have gone into hiding.

Anna suddenly found herself longing for the beautiful twilight of the Polar Nights. Maybe this was why Havski seemed unnerved, too. Something was clearly wrong. Days were always shorter leading up to the Polar Nights, and snow was common, but this weather was . . .

different. Anna just wished she knew for certain whether this was the draugr's doing, and longed to know how to make it go away.

"The sooner we figure out what's really going on, the better," Elsa said, seeming to hear her sister's thoughts as she guided Anna to Havski before helping her up. "I'll be back from Ahtohallan as soon as I can. Then we can decide the best way to handle this."

"Handle this," Anna repeated. *Handle what?* she wondered, and then she remembered. *The draugr! The books in the library! Whether the draugr is Sissel! Right!* Why was she suddenly so forgetful? She didn't want to worry Elsa any more than she had already, so she said nothing about having another foggy moment. Instead, she pulled on Havski's reins. "I'll see you soon. Be careful."

Elsa smiled at her, then whistled for her own steed. The Water Nokk burst through the trees, its crystallized mane casting an array of rainbows across the ground as it raced toward them. Anna watched as Elsa threw her leg over the Water Nokk's back, hoisting herself up. Anna wondered, not for the first time, what it must be like to ride bareback on such a wild creature. Elsa always made it look magical and super comfy, of course.

"Love you!" Elsa smiled at her sister. "See you soon!"

"Love you, too!" Anna called after her as the Water Nokk turned and headed into the forest. Anna watched her sister go, sending out a silent wish for her safety. She hadn't wanted to admit it to Elsa, but she was still shaken by their encounter with the monster the night before. If Elsa hadn't freed her, what would the "D-word" (Anna had decided not to take any chances by saying the creature's full name anymore, just in case!) have done to her?

She shook her head, urging Havski on. No use thinking about what could have happened, she scolded herself. She needed to get back to Arendelle—before something actually did happen.

Once she reached the village, it took all of Anna's strength not to start screaming and waving people down yelling, "Draugr danger!" But she didn't want to terrify everyone. She had to act like a queen, and a queen would remain calm and sound rational. So Anna took a deep breath, deciding she would act firm and direct, and not out of sorts—like she actually was.

It was then she spotted Kristoff, wandering through the town square. "I'm so glad you're here," she said, out of breath.

"What's going on?" Kristoff asked as he reached up to lift Anna off the horse. He helped her down and wrapped his strong arms tightly around her. "Everything okay?"

"We have a situation. I don't want you to panic." *Even if I'm panicking,* she thought. She glanced around at the square, half expecting to see the draugr lurking in the shadows or behind her parents' statue. But no, everything seemed calm. Normal.

"I've learned not to panic till Elsa sends up snow signals," Kristoff joked.

"This is serious," she said, lowering her voice. "We need to warn the village about an impending attack . . . from a draugr." She held her breath, half thinking Kristoff would laugh at her and say she was being as ridiculous as Olaf.

Instead, Kristoff's eyes widened, and she felt his body tighten. "A draugr? Are you serious?"

"Unfortunately, yes. It came out of nowhere when Elsa and I were coming back from Sorenson's. Let's just say we're lucky to be alive." She shivered a little, her mind flashing back to the night before, being trapped by those tree roots. The draugr coming closer and closer . . .

"You saw Sinister Sissel?" Olaf cried out, bounding up beside them. "Did she try to eat you? Did she try to turn you into a draugr, too?" He narrowed his eyes at her, as if trying to determine if she'd been draugrized somehow. "Are you okay, Anna? You can tell me if you're feeling at all monster-y. I won't judge, I swear!"

"I'm fine," Anna insisted. *For now,* she thought. "Look, Olaf, I'm sorry I didn't believe you at first, but I think you might be right. The draugr has to be Sissel— and I think it's behind all the weird weather we've been having."

"I knew it!" Olaf cried, pacing from side to side. "She heard us talking about her at the campfire and now she's come to attack us all. Or at least steal our cheese. And slippers. And possibly our souls." He stared up at the dark sky, opening his mouth and wailing, "Why, Sissel, why?"

"Okay, wait a second. Who is this Sissel again? And why does she want to harm us?" Kristoff asked, looking oddly confused.

Anna did a double take. Had Kristoff just asked who

Sissel was? He was the one who had told them about her to begin with! And now he was acting like he didn't remember her at all! Which was beyond bizarre, considering Kristoff never forgot a thing—even if at times, she wished he would. (Telling him she liked his fish soup was a decision that still haunted her.) This didn't make any sense. Unless . . .

She inhaled sharply as a horrible thought suddenly crossed her mind: could this, too, have something to do with the draugr? Could the draugr—or Sissel—be making them both suddenly so forgetful? There was only one way to find out.

"Quick question," she said to Kristoff. "What very important date for us is coming up?"

Kristoff looked baffled. "Date?"

Olaf slid in next to him. "Just to be clear: there's several."

"Several?" Kristoff parroted.

Anna felt her hands turn clammy. "Having to do with chocolate?" she prompted.

"And the fact you're getting married," Olaf added. "But no one actually knows when yet. You've only been engaged for like a minute."

"Engaged?" Kristoff, looking lost, blinked rapidly.

Anna felt her heart drop. Forgetting their Choco-versary was one thing, but their engagement was implausible.

"Are you feeling okay?" she asked, feeling her anxiety increase.

"Um, Anna?" Olaf tugged on her sleeve. "I hate to be the bearer of bad news, but he's not the only one acting forgetful today. In fact, it's kind of spread to the whole town."

Anna felt her stomach begin to turn. Looking around, it suddenly occurred to her that things were unusually quiet. Everyone was supposed to be working on the Polar Nights festival, yet people seemed to be moving around in a daze. As if they'd forgotten what they were supposed to be doing. Gretchen, the village painter who was meant to be designing the festival banner, was standing in front of a blank canvas with a brush that had no paint on it. Helmut the ice carver was sitting on a solid block of ice, using his ice pick on his teeth!

Anna spotted the baker and hurried over to her. "Hi, Mrs. Blodget!" She sensed she had greeted the older woman with maybe just a little too much cheeriness in her voice. "Just checking in!" she whispered. "How is Kristoff's anniversary chocolate mold coming?"

Mrs. Blodget blinked. "Kristoff's what?"

"Chocolate anniversary gift," Anna said, her uneasy feeling worsening. "You were doing a special order just for me."

"I don't remember any special orders," Mrs. Blodget responded. "But I'm happy to help you with whatever you need."

Anna's heart beat fast in her chest. She turned from Mrs. Blodget to see the two Waffle Brothers standing nearby, not arguing for once. Which was weird in and of itself.

"Hi, guys!" she greeted, her voice now a bit shrill. "What about you? Are you ready for your famous bake-off?"

The brothers looked at one another blankly. "Bake-off? I don't remember signing up for a bake-off," said Bjorn.

"You were going to compete with each other to see who made the better waffle," Anna prompted.

"You make waffles?" Bjarne asked his brother. Bjorn shrugged, taking a bite of a waffle. Anna groaned in frustration.

"It's been like this all morning," Olaf said nervously. "The choir couldn't remember the lyrics to their songs, the pie maker forgot to bake his piecrusts, and the candle shop couldn't find their wax."

"Are you serious?" Anna asked. This was getting worse and worse. She leaned against a lamppost, feeling like the world was spinning out of control. "The draugr," she whispered. "This all has to be from the draugr." She closed her eyes for a moment, hearing the creature's moan in her mind.

Sissssttterrrr.

"It must have come here last night and stolen everyone's memories." She squeezed her eyes shut even tighter. "What am I going to do?"

"You could try to stop it?" Olaf suggested brightly. "I mean, just a thought!"

"But how?"

"At the campfire, you mentioned a book about draugrs you found in your parents' secret library," Olaf reminded her. Clearly, he wasn't suffering from the same memory loss the rest of them were experiencing. "You might start there."

Of course! Anna smacked her forehead with her

hand. That was why she'd come back to Arendelle to begin with! To research draugrs! She'd totally forgotten.

Again.

Oh, dear.

"Olaf, we need to find that book right away!" Anna cried, grabbing both his hand and Kristoff's for safekeeping.

She started to pull them toward the castle, then stopped.

There was one thing she had to do first. Anna let go of Kristoff's hand temporarily, grabbed a piece of paper and a pencil off a nearby table, and scribbled a quick note. Then she held it up in the air.

"Gale?" she called out, and then waited. No matter where the Wind Spirit was when she called, it always seemed to respond quickly, and this time was no different. Gale whisked through the street, blowing unhung decorations for the festival along with it. Anna let the note ride on the wind. "Find my sister and get her back to Arendelle as fast as you can!"

CHAPTER NINE

Elsa

"AH, AH, AH, AH . . ."

Elsa couldn't help singing as she and the Water Nokk approached Ahtohallan. It was her version of greeting the Mother Spirit embodied in the glacier. Ahtohallan had become like a second home to her over the last two months. Well, not a home, exactly. But a place of peace. Just being there centered her somehow. She found the icy surroundings comforting. It didn't really make any sense when she tried to explain it to her sister. But Anna was always so supportive and understanding—even when she didn't quite get it. It was a sister thing, she surmised.

She wished she could take Anna here. But there was

no way to cross the Dark Sea without the Water Nokk, and the spirit had a mind of its own. Which was why Elsa was working so hard to bring the memories home to share with her sister. So Anna could catch just a glimpse of the mysteries revealed here in this fortress of ice.

Because, oh, she'd seen so much in her short time here. She'd gone deep, as deep as she dared, watching her family's history unfold in front of her eyes. Seeing her mother save her father's life in the Enchanted Forest. Watching them grow up together, become friends, fall in love. Witness the pain her mother had gone through keeping the secret that she was Northuldra. Elsa knew all too well about keeping secrets.

And then there were the moments that were harder to watch. The fear in her father's eyes as he witnessed young Elsa's magic grow. He loved her so much—he tried his best—but he had also grown up with secrets. And he, too, had learned to adhere to the horrific mantra, "Conceal, don't feel." He'd passed that on to her, thinking he was doing the best thing he could to help her keep the kingdom. Would he have approved if he knew she'd given it all to Anna in the end after all? Deep down, she believed he would. He would have done anything to keep his girls safe and happy.

And she *was* happy, she thought, as she slid off the Water Spirit and stepped up to the icy entrance. She was living free in the Enchanted Forest, no longer imprisoned by her guilt and fear. She now had everything she had never known she wanted—*needed*. She had peace. She had power.

And yet she still had her sister. And Arendelle.

Elsa was blown away by how gracious the kingdom had been the day she gave up her throne. She thought they'd be furious with her. She thought they'd believe she was abandoning them. But no—they understood that she needed this. That she had given them everything she could over the past three years. And now it was time for her to give herself something, too. Something she desperately needed to become the best version of herself. And so, when she had stood on that dais in front of all of Arendelle—and the cheers and shouts of encouragement rose to her ears—she felt tears of gratitude slip down her cheeks. They truly loved her; not just as their queen, but as a person—a citizen of Arendelle!

They were willing to let her go, and because of that she would never truly leave them.

Elsa's steps quickened as she raced down the icy path, deeper into Ahtohallan. The walls shimmered in their greeting to her, flickering with images of her mother smiling down at her as she ran. Ahtohallan was a mother herself—the mother of all the other spirits. And she often embodied echoes of Elsa's own mother, Queen Iduna, to give Elsa a friendly face to come home to. And while Elsa knew it was not really her mother in those icy ripples on the wall—her mother was long gone—she still couldn't keep her heart from swelling with love as she gazed upon the vision of the woman who had given birth to her. Who had loved her unconditionally. Who had believed her powers to be a gift, not a curse. Who had sacrificed her life to try to save her.

At last Elsa stepped into the cavernous heart of the glacier. The icy walls stretched tall above her, as far as her eyes could see, reflecting memories that danced on their surfaces. Ahtohallan was the keeper of memories. And memories were knowledge. There was so much knowledge bursting within these walls—more than any mere library could possibly hold. Surely, she could find something to help with their current situation. The strange darkness, the storms, the draugr that had attacked Anna. And then there were her powers, which had seemed to fizzle out for no reason as she'd attempted to pull a memory up for her sister.

No. Elsa shook her head, her white-blond hair shimmering under the icy lights. *No, it wasn't just that they fizzled out.*

It was as if she'd forgotten the memory altogether.

Just like everyone else had been forgetting things. She thought back to the night by the campfire. Kristoff had watched his tent go down—and then seemed to forget all about it a moment later. And then there was the next night in the shepherd's hut, right after the draugr encounter. Anna had been so excited about seeing Elsa's memory—but then seemed to lose all interest. And the next morning she hadn't remembered anything they'd talked about doing.

But was it simply forgetfulness? Or was the loss of memory connected to the draugr somehow? Was Anna's hunch correct? Was the draugr Sissel, reawakened by Kristoff's story on the anniversary of her death?

Elsa pressed a hand against the cold wall of ice, trying

to concentrate. Trying again to find that memory she'd wanted to share with Anna, of her father and mother laughing and dancing in the ballroom. She'd pulled it up a hundred times before—it was one of her favorites.

But this time, it didn't materialize.

"What's wrong?" she whispered, though she knew the glacier couldn't answer. "Where's the memory? Why can't I access it?"

A taste of dread rose in her throat. What was going on here? And was it connected somehow to everything else? After all, it was one thing for Kristoff or Anna to start forgetting things. But quite another for the very literal glacier of memories. Heart beating fast, Elsa pressed her other hand against the icy wall, drawing in a deep but shaky breath.

"Just try something else," she told herself. "Father under his favorite tree. Mother popping down from the branches, upside down and surprising him." Another favorite. One she'd pulled up many times before.

For a moment, she thought she saw something. A flicker in the ice, the beginnings of a memory forming. But then it fizzled out as it had in the shepherd's hut. The ice swirled, then grew dark again.

The memory was gone. As if it had been stolen away from her.

But just as she began to despair, the walls of Ahtohallan suddenly seemed to brighten and shimmer. A gray mist began to rise into the air. A moment later, sculptures made of ice solidified in front of her. But they were not of her mother or her father and their favorite tree. Rather, they were two girls—around Anna and Elsa's age—wearing clothing that looked old-fashioned. As Elsa watched, the ice began to shift, expand, revealing their location. They were standing on a riverbank.

And they were arguing bitterly.

Elsa gaped. Could it be . . . ? Her mind flashed back to Kristoff's story of the Vesterland sisters.

One day, Inger got her wish. While on a trip to Arendelle, she caught her sister standing by the rushing river—alone.

"What is this?" she whispered, fear crawling down her spine. Half of her wanted to look away. To turn and flee the glacier altogether and never look back. But instead, something compelled her to stay as the memory swirled and the ice sculptures seemed to come to life. The river rising. Raging. One of the girls being swept away in its vicious current, thrashing in the water, screaming for help.

"*INGER!*" The words seemed to echo through the icy walls. "*Inger—help me!*" The vision swirled again, now focusing on the second girl. She was on her knees by the riverbank, her eyes flowing with tears.

"*Sissel,*" she croaked. "*I'm so sorry, Sissel!*"

The vision froze; the moving figures were now just statues in the ice. Elsa dropped to her own knees, overwhelmed by what she'd just seen. It was one thing to hear about what happened long ago. But it was quite another to see Sissel thrashing in the rough waters, begging her sister for help while Inger was motionless on the riverbank, clearly filled with remorse for her evil deed.

Elsa didn't feel sorry for her, though. She deserved all she had gotten and more. But poor Sissel! Elsa couldn't imagine what must have gone through her mind in those last seconds. The realization that her own sister had hated her enough—had been jealous enough—to do such a thing.

Suddenly she felt a gust of wind behind her. She whirled around, surprised to find Gale swooping into the glacier, a piece of mail in its breeze. She plucked the letter from the Wind Spirit and opened it, her hands still trembling from all she'd seen.

It was from Anna.

Something is very wrong in Arendelle. You need to come back—as soon as possible—before it's too late!

CHAPTER TEN

Anna

KRISTOFF MIGHT HAVE BEEN CONFUSED about a few things, but one thing he remembered was his love of lingonberry pie. Leaving him and Sven in the capable hands of Olina, the castle cook, who had a fresh pie hot out of the oven, Anna and Olaf trudged up to the secret room that led to her parents' private library.

Anna pulled on the Water Nokk statue that guarded the space and the bookcase swung open, revealing the arched passageway beyond. She and Olaf stepped inside. Anna stifled a sneeze as they headed down the passageway into the windowless secret room. It was still a bit dusty, though she had tried to clear out all the cobwebs that had draped the bookcases. Before she'd discovered the room, it had been years since anyone had used it, making it a perfect home for spiders and other small creatures of the castle that Anna didn't really want to run into. But she'd shooed them all away, knowing her mother would have approved of a clean home—everywhere.

She paused at the entrance to the room, taking in the high shelves filled with books and scrolls and other curios—glass beakers, silver scales. A portrait of Aren of Arendelle, the legendary ruler of Arendelle of old, hung from a far wall. The place probably didn't look much different now from how it had when her parents had first stumbled upon it in their teens. According to Elsa's Ahtohallan memories, this room had been a special place for Iduna and Agnarr. A secret hideaway where they could spend time together without anyone else watching. A perfect place to fall in love.

Anna sighed dreamily over her parents' romance, then got back to the task at hand, heading straight to the bookshelves. Her fingers flew over the leather spines, looking for the book she remembered reading one time, about mythical creatures that went bump in the night.

Or bump in the day that resembled the night. But where was it?

"Come out, come out, wherever you are, book," Anna muttered, staring at all the tomes in front of her. Their spines boasted tales of the history of Arendelle and information about the science of soil, and there were even some fun mysteries thrown in for good measure. But nothing about draugrs. She sighed and moved to another shelf. Surely, it had to be here somewhere.

"I think I found it!" Olaf exclaimed at last, from the top of the ladder. He pulled an old, cracked leather book from the very top shelf and tossed it to the floor. It landed with a loud thump, stirring up a large cloud of dust, which made him sneeze. "It was stuck behind a book on the history of cheese." He giggled. "How cheesy is that?" He jumped off the ladder to retrieve the book, then shuffled over to the table.

"That's it!" Anna said, feeling relieved when she saw the title: *Of Nightmares and Nixies*. She stepped up to the table and cracked open the spine, causing more dust to float into the air in the low-lit space. She skimmed through it until she found a page titled "Draugrs." A sketch of a creepy-looking creature in tattered clothing, skin practically peeling off its body, stared back at them. Anna shuddered at the sight. "That's what I ran into, all right."

" 'A draugr,' " Olaf read, " 'is sometimes thought of as a ghost or spirit but is in fact a reanimated, decayed corpse that rose from the dead because it didn't receive a proper burial.' "

The two looked at one another and said, "Eww," at the same time.

"Also," Olaf observed, "that fits Sinister Sissel! She drowned, remember?"

Anna felt a prickling at the back of her neck, thinking back to the creature towering over her in the woods while she lay on the ground, its blackened teeth bared. Princess Sissel—come back from the dead. "Let's keep reading," she said, pushing her fears aside. "It says here that draugrs can have magical abilities and can control the weather and turn day into night." She grimaced. "Well, we know that part already!"

Olaf pointed to another passage. "And here's where it talks about memories. Draugrs have the power to slip in and steal people's memories while they sleep." He flipped the page. "But where's the part about stealing slippers? That seems important."

Anna's heartbeat quickened. "So the draugr *did* come to Arendelle while Elsa and I were gone. And it stole everyone's memories!"

"But why?" Olaf asked, looking up from the book.

Anna scowled, squeezing her hands into fists. "I know why. Sissel is mad at me for becoming queen in place of Elsa. She doesn't know the whole story, and now she's taking it out on the kingdom!" She shook her head. "What we need to find out is whether the memories the draugr stole are gone for good or if there's a way to get them back. Does the book say anything about that?" She flipped the pages anxiously, but the words seemed to blur. It was then that she became aware that she was crying.

"Anna, are you okay?" Olaf asked, concerned.

She wasn't, Anna realized. She wasn't okay at all. "What if their memory loss gets worse?" she said worriedly. "Right now, Kristoff can't even remember our engagement. If we don't get rid of this draugr, he

could end up forgetting everything . . . including me."
Her voice caught on the last part. She couldn't imagine
a world where Kristoff didn't know her. Didn't *love* her.

Olaf patted her hand. "Don't worry, Anna. We won't
let that happen. I'm sure if we can just get rid of the
draugr, everything will go back to normal. And look!"
He pointed at the next page in the book. "They even list
ways to do it."

"They do?" Anna asked, a glimmer of hope rising
inside her. She scanned the passage Olaf had pointed to
quickly. Then she frowned. "Uh, it says we can chop off
its head . . ."

The snowman shrugged. "Brutal. But likely effective."

"And likely impossible," Anna muttered. She
thought back to the encounter the night before and tried
to imagine even getting close enough to the corpse to
remove its head. "There's got to be something else." She
turned back to the book, her eyes focusing on a paragraph
on the next page. "Okay, what about this? It says if you
can lead the draugr back into its grave, it will find peace
and fade away."

"Well, that does seem much less violent," Olaf
agreed, looking a little relieved.

"Except . . . Sissel doesn't have a grave. She was swept out to sea." Anna tried not to panic. This was proving to be harder than she'd thought.

"I wonder if Elsa could freeze the draugr and then shatter it into a thousand pieces," Olaf mused. "Ice powers . . . swoosh!"

Hmm. Anna consulted the book again. A moment later, she shook her head. "I don't think that'll work, either. It says here draugrs are immune to acts of strength. In fact, it says that when angered, they can curse their enemies and prevent them from growing stronger." She pursed her lips. "Back in the forest, Elsa made it really mad by making this wall of ice. And immediately afterward, her powers started fizzling out."

"That doesn't seem good," Olaf murmured.

"No." Anna sighed, closing the book. "This is not good at all."

"What isn't?" called out a new voice.

Anna looked up just in time to see Elsa burst into the room. Her sister leaned on her hands and knees, trying to catch her breath. "I got your note and came as fast as I could."

Anna ran around the table, throwing her arms around

her sister. "I'm so glad to see you. We're too late to stop the draugr. It's already been here and stolen people's memories!"

Elsa's face was pained. "No. Oh, Anna . . . are you sure?"

Anna grimaced. "Unfortunately, yes. Even Kristoff's . . ." She trailed off, miserable as her mind flashed to her handsome ice harvester. "And that's not all—the book says draugrs can curse their enemies and prevent them from growing stronger." She looked at Elsa. "Do you think that's why your powers started to fizzle after we saw the draugr?"

Elsa sat down on one of the velvet chairs, looking drained. "Maybe. I was having trouble pulling up memories from Ahtohallan, too. I didn't understand why. But now . . ." She closed her eyes.

"I don't believe this is happening," Anna said, feeling worse.

Elsa's eyes flew open. "There was something else. Wow, I just remembered."

Was Elsa's memory on the fritz, too? Anna didn't dare ask her about her powers.

"What is it?" she pressed.

"In Ahtohallan. *Our* memories were missing. But there was something new in their place. One I'd never seen before. A memory of Sissel and Inger."

Anna was startled. Ahtohallan held memories of the Vesterland sisters? She supposed that made sense—after all, the world was a lot bigger than just Arendelle. But could those memories hold a clue to any of this mess? "What did you see?" she asked, breath caught in her throat.

"I saw Sissel get swept away in the river, and Inger crying on the riverbank and calling to her," Elsa said. "I know it doesn't make sense."

"No." Anna's hope faded. "Why would Inger be calling to her sister if she pushed her in?"

"I don't know," Elsa replied. "Guilt, maybe? For harming her own sister?" Elsa held her arms tightly around her chest. "It's too awful to even think about, let alone see it. But the strange thing was, I didn't call up the memory. It just appeared. Meanwhile, memories I know I've seen before—like of Mother and Father reading by their favorite tree—have disappeared. I couldn't even recover them when I tried."

"I think this is all Sissel's doing," Anna said, feeling

helpless. She quickly filled Elsa in on everything else she and Olaf had read.

"So a draugr is almost impossible to destroy, is causing this strange weather, and might have stolen my powers and some of our memories," Elsa summed up.

"And it wants to turn Anna into a draugr," Olaf added, presumably trying to be helpful. He looked quizzically at Anna. "Hey, when's the last time you saw your slippers?"

Anna felt the anger building inside her again. They had a lot of information and still didn't know what to do with it. Luckily, she knew someone who might be able to help them. He'd been able to point them in the right direction before. Anna looked at her sister. "We have to go see Grand Pabbie and the trolls. Maybe they can help us figure out how to destroy this monster before it's too late."

CHAPTER ELEVEN

Elsa

BY THE TIME THEY LEFT the castle the next morning, it had started snowing hard, but Elsa knew there was no time to lose. They had to get to the trolls as fast as they could. They packed everything they needed for their journey into Kristoff's sled, including Kristoff himself. There was no way Anna was going to leave him unattended for that long with his memory loss. ("What if he forgets what cliffs are and jumps off one? What if he eats poison mushrooms, thinking they're ingredients for Flemmingrad stew?")

Olaf insisted on coming, too, and so the four of

them—led by Sven, who thankfully still seemed to remember how to pull a sled—headed out of town, toward the Valley of the Living Rock, where the trolls made their home.

The cold rarely bothered Elsa, of course, but it sure seemed to be affecting everyone else in the party as they made their way up the steep mountainside. And even she had to admit that she didn't appreciate the snow and ice that had started piling up on the ground and making it difficult to maneuver the sled up the narrow trails— especially when it was practically pitch dark around them. The sun still hadn't made an appearance, and if anything, the sky had gotten even bleaker since the lights first winked out two days before. Even their torches couldn't seem to make a great dent in the darkness.

"Where are we going again?" Kristoff asked for the thousandth time. He looked up at Anna from his seat in the back of the sled, scratching his head. "Are we headed to the North Mountain to find your crazy sister?"

Anna groaned. Elsa could tell she was getting frustrated with him. "No, Kristoff. We already did that. Remember?"

"Yeah, of course I remember," Kristoff replied. He peered at Elsa, who was sitting up front with Anna. "Who are you again?"

Elsa gave him a bland smile. "The crazy sister?"

Anna groaned again. "Please don't make it worse."

"I'm sorry." Elsa put a hand on Anna's knee and squeezed it comfortingly. "I know you're worried about him. But it'll be okay. I know it will. The trolls are masters at manipulating memories, remember?"

"Actually, I don't," Anna said with a sigh. "Since they took a lot of mine."

"Right. Sorry. Again." Elsa stared out into the dark night, gnawing on her lower lip. Way to stick her foot in her mouth.

"No, *I'm* sorry," Anna replied, giving Elsa a rueful look. "I know you're just trying to make me feel better. It's just . . . this is so awful. I mean, look at him." She gestured to Kristoff, who was staring at Olaf with frank fascination.

"Whoa," he whispered. "Is that a snowman?"

"I'm Olaf," Olaf said gently. "I like warm hugs?"

"A talking snowman?" Kristoff exclaimed. "Now

that is just weird." He turned to Anna. "Where are we going again?"

Anna moaned. Elsa pulled her into her arms. "Don't worry," she assured her. "The trolls are going to fix him right up! We just have to get there." She peered at her sister's face. "How are *you* doing?" she asked. "Are you feeling . . . fuzzy?" It was bad enough Kristoff and half of Arendelle had lost their minds. If Anna started going, too . . .

"A little," Anna admitted, scrunching up her nose. "But definitely not as bad as everyone else. Maybe because we weren't in Arendelle the other night, we escaped the worst of it."

"And I don't feel anything at all!" Olaf proclaimed. "Sharp as a tack! Smart as a whip! It's probably because water has memory," he confided to the girls.

"Strangely, you might be right . . ." Elsa mused.

"I usually am," declared Olaf. He paused dramatically. "Or don't you *remember*?"

"Whoa!" Kristoff exclaimed, peering at Olaf. "What are you?"

"Snowman. Talking. Yes, it's weird." Anna turned to Elsa. "Are we almost there yet?"

"Not really," Elsa said apologetically, her eyes traveling down the steep mountain as the wind picked up, causing the snow to swirl around them and sting her eyes. Arendelle was so far away that it looked like a toy village. But they still had a long way to go. And by the looks of their shivering selves, she wasn't sure they were going to make it without a stop to warm up.

It was then that she saw a light in the distance. Just a flicker, but something was definitely there. "What is that?" she asked, squinting. "Someone's house?" Maybe if they were home, they'd let them warm up by the fire for a few minutes. She was pretty sure she still had a few marshmallows in her satchel, too.

Anna's eyes lit up as she tracked the light. "No! I think that's Oaken's Trading Post!" She shot an excited look at her sister. "Which means . . ."

"Sauna!" they said in unison.

"Come on, Sven!" Anna called to the reindeer. "Last one to the sauna is a rotten snowman!"

"Fun fact! Snowmen don't rot! They melt!" Olaf remarked as Sven picked up the pace, charging toward the light. From the way he was galloping, Elsa wondered if he might still remember Oaken's usual carrot stash under the counter. Fortunately, the reindeer didn't seem to be losing his memory along with everyone else. Maybe animals were immune, like snowmen.

A few moments later they were out of the sleigh and standing at the hut, with Oaken in the doorway, giving them a warm, welcoming grin. The burly redheaded proprietor was wearing an incredibly ugly-on-purpose Polar Nights sweater complete with a rainbow-yarn replica of the aurora borealis on the front.

"Hoo-hoo! Great to see you, Your Majesties!" he declared. "Real howler in December, *ja*? Come in before you freeze to death!" He opened the door wide, and they gratefully stepped inside the shop. The warmth hit them immediately and they all let out loud sighs of relief. Even Elsa had to admit it felt good to be out of the cold.

Taking off her cloak, she looked around. The store was all decked out for the upcoming Polar Nights festivities, complete with crates of Polar Night party kits, which appeared to contain an assortment of sparklers, special goggles to view the Northern Lights, and very silly socks. They didn't, however, appear to be a very popular item: kits were piled from floor to ceiling. Which could have been due to the recent bad weather, Elsa concluded.

Or . . . she surmised, glancing at the tag on one of the kits, maybe it was just the price. . . .

"Come!" Oaken instructed, opening the door at the back of the shop. A blast of hot air roared into the small space, and they all sighed dreamily. "Let's warm you up!"

A few minutes later they had all changed into white fluffy robes and packed into the small, steamy sauna. Even Olaf, thanks to his permafrost, was able to relax on the bench, a towel splayed across his lap. "Ahh," he said, closing his eyes. "This feels just like summer."

"Have I been here before?" Kristoff squinted at Oaken. "Are we friends?"

Oaken raised an eyebrow. "Is he all right?" he asked, turning to the women.

"Not exactly," Anna said. "There's something strange going on in Arendelle. That's why we're out here in this storm. We're going to see the trolls in hopes they can clear some of it up."

"*Ja!* I need this weather to clear up soon!" Oaken agreed, frowning. "I've had no customers for days! Usually this is my busiest season! But now—it's like people forgot I was here!"

"There may be more to that idea than you know,"

Elsa replied. "A lot of people in Arendelle have been experiencing missing memories, just like Kristoff here. It's very strange." She wasn't sure she should mention the draugr. She didn't want to worry the shopkeeper.

Oaken shifted in his seat, looking suddenly uncomfortable. "Well, that seems rather bad," he said. "I hope my family is okay. They journeyed to Arendelle three days ago to attend the Polar Nights parties. I had been planning to join them once I sold all our party kits."

"Might be time to have a sale," said Olaf, looking at the large stack of kits, more of which were piled in the corner of the sauna.

"We can definitely check on your family when we get back," Elsa assured him. "Once we figure out what's going on."

Oaken nodded solemnly. "And you think the trolls can help with that?"

"Sorenson seemed to think so," Elsa said. "And honestly, we don't have a lot of other options."

"The trolls are very wise. Surely, they will be able to help you," Oaken agreed. He paused, then added, "Did you know Grand Pabbie came here once? He bought all my spring mushrooms—at full price, too!"

He pointed to a wall of portraits across the sauna that Elsa hadn't noticed before. Paintings of all the famous people who had visited the sauna, she guessed.

"Ooh! There's us! And our parents!" Anna said, pointing to a cute picture of her and Elsa hanging next to one of King Agnarr and Queen Iduna, alongside other neighboring nobles. "Ugh. And there's Hans," she added, screwing up her face as she noticed the picture of her ex-fiancé—who was hopefully still rotting away in the Southern Islands. "What a bad likeness," she added. "He's really not that tall, you know. Or good-looking. Also, his nose is way bigger. And crookeder—"

"Is that me?" Kristoff interrupted, pointing to the next wall over, where there were more portraits—these under a sign that read BANNED FROM THE TRADING POST. Sure enough, there was a rough sketch of Kristoff, with an ugly scowl on his face, waving a fistful of carrots menacingly. Elsa stifled a giggle. Kristoff might not remember, but he and Oaken had a bit of an unpleasant history. Guess they were lucky the redheaded proprietor hadn't left him out in the cold.

"Uh, sorry!" Oaken said, his cheeks turning red, as Anna shot him a look. "That needs to be updated now that you're going to be a member of the royal family." He leapt from his seat and ran over to the sketch, scrawling *Okay!* over Kristoff's face in red ink. He glanced at Kristoff for a moment, then added *For now!* underneath.

Anna shook her head. Elsa smiled, going back to the original set of portraits to continue to look for Pabbie amongst them. Instead, her eyes locked on a portrait of two young girls, one with long braided hair and the other with a short bob. They had their arms around each other and were smiling happily. Something uneasy twisted in her stomach.

"Are those the . . ." she started.

"The famous Vesterland princesses!" Oaken finished for her. "*Ja!* They used to stop here with their parents on their way back home after trips. My father was only a boy back then, and they used to play together. He was always talking about how sweet they were. How close." He smiled at Elsa and Anna. "Just like the two of you."

"That can't be right," Anna interjected. "Sissel and Inger hated each other." She turned to Elsa. "I'm right, right? It's not my memory going on the fritz again?"

Elsa shook her head. "No. You're correct. Inger hated Sissel because she wanted the crown for herself."

"Inger wanted to be queen?" Oaken asked, looking confused. "My father said she wanted to be a scientist. He said she was always digging in the dirt and talking about soil." He laughed. "My dad said it was quite boring how she'd go on and on about nature and protecting natural habitats for animals."

"Inger was into protecting nature?" Anna asked. "That's interesting. No one mentioned that to us before." She glanced over at Elsa, and Elsa could practically see the wheels turning in her younger sister's head. "I wonder if there's more to this story than we know."

Elsa shrugged. "Maybe. But first we have more important things to focus on."

Like a monster on the loose. And missing memories. For now, the story of those two sisters had to take a backseat.

Elsa rose to her feet, wiping the sweat from her brow.

"Okay, warm-up over," she declared. "Let's go find the trolls."

Elsa couldn't be sure anymore whether it was day or night as they walked up the steep slope that led to the

Valley of the Living Rock. They'd parked the sleigh at the bottom of the hill—no way was it going to make it up the last bit of that incline. Plus, it was so dark up here, they'd needed to buy new torches from Oaken just to be able to navigate the steep, narrow path without accidentally falling off a cliff in the process.

Fortunately, Olaf was enjoying himself so much at the sauna, they'd convinced him to sit this part of the trip out. He was hesitant at first, but the moment he and Oaken started singing Polar Nights carols, he'd decided it was for the best as well. Too cold out there! Nothing at all like summer!

Elsa had suggested leaving Kristoff, too, but Anna wouldn't hear of it. The trolls were his found family—and experts in memory loss, too. If anyone could help him, it would be them. (Also, she didn't really trust him not to start a fight with Oaken and get kicked out into the cold.)

They rounded the corner, stepping into the valley. Elsa was relieved to see the nocturnal trolls were awake and pretty busy with what looked like party preparations. The valley was decorated with moss and vines, and glowing crystals were strategically lighting up the space, giving it a beautiful golden glow. The trolls themselves were decked out in mossy capes—each one more elaborate than the last. There was even a very interesting sculpture of the famous Flemmingrad in the center of the valley, a troll effigy made of a mixture of mushrooms and moss residing above a foul-smelling pot of stew.

"Your Majesties!" cried a young troll, running toward them. He threw his arms around Anna's knees, almost knocking her over in the process. He was small, but clearly heavy as a rock. "It's so good to see you! Have you come for the Crystal Ceremony?"

Elsa immediately recognized Little Rock, whom they'd helped a few years back during his own Crystal Ceremony, a special celebration where young trolls earned their crystals by mastering skills such as tracking, harvesting, and stargazing.

"There are five trolls earning their crystals this year," Little Rock told the group proudly. "And I'm helping the ones who are having problems. Just like you once helped me." He peered from Elsa to Anna to Kristoff. "Did you come to help, too?"

Elsa shook her head. "I'm afraid not," she apologized. "We're here on much more serious matters. Is Grand Pabbie around, by chance?" She scanned the valley. There were so many trolls wandering about in the dark that it was hard to make out who was who.

Before Little Rock could answer, a new troll rolled up to the group and popped open. It was Bulda, the female troll who had raised Kristoff from the time he was a little boy. She was dressed quite fancifully in a long mossy gown strewn with colorful flowers. Her face broke out into a rocky grin when her eyes fell on her adopted son.

"Kristoff," she cried happily. "You've come to visit old Bulda! And . . ." Her gaze turned to Anna and her toothy smile widened. "You brought your bride, too! Are you two fixer-uppers *finally* ready to get married? Because we can do it now! I mean, yes, we're a little busy preparing for the Crystal Ceremony and all, but we will always make time for true love." She beamed at Kristoff.

"Um," Kristoff stammered, staring down at the troll with a confounded look on his face. "Who are you? *What* are you? 'Cause you look like a rock, no offense." He scratched his head and started wandering aimlessly across the field. "Talking snowmen. Talking rocks . . ." Elsa heard him mutter under his breath. "What's next? A talking reindeer?"

Behind him, Sven snorted. Anna face-palmed.

Bulda raised a bushy eyebrow, turning questioningly to Anna. The queen gave the troll an apologetic look. "Let's just say he's not exactly himself today," she told the troll in a hushed voice. "It's actually part of the reason we're here. That and the strange weather."

"Ah, yes. The weather."

The group whirled around to find Grand Pabbie himself waddling over toward them. He was wearing his fancy ceremonial moss cape, and his neck was draped with so many crystals that Elsa found herself wondering how he didn't tip over. He gave them a grave look.

"I was hoping you'd come," he said. "I wanted to come to you, but this is a busy time for us, as you know. If we miss the Northern Lights, these young trolls will have to wait another year to earn their crystals."

"And we're sorry to disturb you," Elsa said, dropping down to her knees to be at eye level with the troll. "But we didn't know where else to turn. Something is very wrong in Arendelle. The darkness. The storms. People forgetting things. This is not your typical Polar Nights." She pursed her lips. "We think it might be the work of a draugr."

She paused, half expecting Grand Pabbie to laugh at her foolishness. To tell her what was happening wasn't magical at all and that there was a very logical explanation for all of it. But instead, his face grew even more serious as he absently fingered a large red crystal hanging from his neck.

"A draugr," he mused. "Yes. That would explain a lot. But draugrs don't just come out of nowhere. When did you first see it?"

Elsa frowned. She and Anna had seen it in the woods on the way back from Sorenson's. But Kristoff and Olaf had sworn they'd seen something the night of the campfire. The night Kristoff had told the story.

The night Inger had killed Sissel—fifty years before.

"We were telling scary stories," she said. "And Kristoff told one about a draugr who was once a princess." She bit her lower lip. "Do you think somehow we could have accidentally summoned a draugr by talking about it?"

"Names can have power," Grand Pabbie agreed

solemnly. "It could be that you got its attention with your story and angered it somehow."

"I think it's angry at me," Anna piped in. "Though for a totally unjustified reason!"

Grand Pabbie cocked his head, seemingly perplexed. "What are you saying?"

"We think the draugr was once a princess from Vesterland who was going to be queen," Elsa explained. "But she was killed by her younger sister, who wanted the crown. Anna thinks because she's also a younger sister—who became queen—that the draugr wants to punish her, since she can't get revenge on her actual murderer."

"It's true! It read the *Village Crown* story about me," Anna added. "And then it started shrieking 'Sister!' Like, I'm the same as its sister."

Grand Pabbie nodded sagely. "I can see why you might make that connection. But there is one important difference."

"What's that?" Anna asked.

"You did not kill your sister."

"Oh. Right." Anna looked sheepish. "Good point."

"Draugrs are very simple creatures," Grand Pabbie added. "They usually come back from the dead for one purpose. One unfinished task. One regret. Something about their past they hope to correct." He leveled his eyes on Anna and Elsa. "Not to seek revenge on total strangers."

Elsa let out a breath of relief. Well, that was something, she supposed. Though it didn't really clear things up. "So why did it appear after we told the story? And what does it want?" she asked, feeling a little hopeless.

Grand Pabbie seemed to consider this for a moment. "Perhaps the stars can tell us something," he said at last. Elsa watched, heart in her throat, as he waved his hand in the air and the clouds above them parted, revealing a shiny sky of stars so beautiful it took Elsa's breath away. She hadn't realized how much she'd missed the night sky in the last few days. The simple joy of looking up and seeing an entire universe shining back at you. The troll's eyes took on a faraway look, as if he were going into a trance. After a moment, he opened his mouth to speak.

"What once did flee, now sets sail," he intoned. *"To end this all, you must tell her tale."*

"What?" Elsa asked, confused. What kind of riddle was that? "Do you mean the sisters' tale? But Kristoff already told that! It's what started this whole thing to begin with."

"I'm afraid the answers aren't so simple," Grand Pabbie said.

"Meaning?" Elsa tried, but Grand Pabbie said nothing.

"Grand Pabbie?" Anna tried again. "What aren't you telling us?"

Elsa watched as the clouds swept back in as quickly as they had parted, the sky growing bleak and black once again. The elder troll dropped his gaze from the heavens and turned back to the two queens, his rocky face as solemn as the grave.

"If you fail to set things right, day will forever be cast into night."

CHAPTER TWELVE

Anna

ANNA WAS TOO STUNNED TO SPEAK.

She couldn't believe what she was hearing. Forever night? The kingdom plunged into eternal darkness? Not to mention never-ending storms! What would they do if that happened? Without the sun, Arendelle's crops would wither and die. Ships would sink in the stormy waters of the sea instead of reaching safe harbor with their medicines and supplies. She didn't want to believe what Grand Pabbie was saying, but he'd never been wrong about something like this.

And then there was another horrifying question needling at her, begging for an answer. One she wasn't sure she really wanted to ask. Because while storms were bad and eternal night was worse . . .

Memories . . . people's memories . . .

"Grand Pabbie?" she ventured, her tone softening. "If we can't rid Arendelle of this threat—"

"We will," Elsa cut in firmly.

"But if we *can't*," Anna continued gently, "does that mean . . . could it also mean . . ."

Her voice caught as she stared across the valley at the burly ice harvester and his reindeer. Kristoff was taking in the sight of the talking, rolling, jumping trolls in amazement, as if he'd never seen them before. Even Sven was looking at him strangely. "Will the people . . . will Kristoff . . ."

"I'm sorry, Anna," Grand Pabbie replied, his voice equally soft. He didn't have to continue.

Anna forced herself to focus on the crystals around the trolls' necks, hoping the illuminating colors would calm her. All she wanted to do was scream. Why did Kristoff have to tell that scary story? Why?

"But you must know some spell, or remedy, that can help people with their lost memories," she insisted, her voice escalating in volume. "You've removed memories before. You must know how to put them back in, too!"

Then again, she thought begrudgingly, the trolls never did recover all *her* erased memories, which they'd removed when she was a child to protect her from her sister's magic. To this day, her mind still had holes in it, precious missing moments of time spent with her sister she'd never get back.

Grand Pabbie's eyes flitted to Kristoff across the valley. "I am sorry, Your Majesty. Our own ways are hard enough to control. Trying to master another's is almost impossible. I cannot undo what the draugr has done."

"But that means . . . Kristoff," Anna's voice caught on the name. She thought of the mountain man who had stolen her heart with his love of ice, with the way he spoke on his reindeer's behalf, with his enthusiastic love of unusual recipes.

Kristoff. *Her Kristoff.*

Memories flashed through her mind. The first time they'd kissed after she'd presented him with his new sled, the first time they'd played charades. The moment he had gotten down on one knee and asked her to marry him.

Kristoff—*her* Kristoff! Who could now barely remember who she was.

Anna felt her legs buckle. The trolls and Elsa reached for her, but Anna stepped back, unwilling to be helped.

No. She wasn't willing to accept that Kristoff's love for her could disappear because of some creature's doing. And she wasn't about to let her people suffer from eternal night or never-ending storms, either. She was queen of Arendelle. It was her job to fix this.

Somehow.

Her mind raced, trying to remember Grand Pabbie's words as he'd consulted with the stars. The troll spoke in riddles. But there was usually a clue buried within them.

What once did flee, now sets sail . . .
To end this all, you must tell her tale . . .

Her tale. But they'd told Sissel's tale! At the campfire. And again in Arendelle . . .

Suddenly, Anna's mind flashed back to Oaken's sauna as they were looking at the portraits of the two princesses. How Oaken had insisted Inger and Sissel were friends, not enemies as Kristoff and the others had claimed. He'd also sworn that Inger had wanted to be a scientist, not a queen like her sister. At the time, Anna had wondered if there could be more to their story.

Now she was convinced there must be.

She turned to Elsa, her face showing her determination.

"The answer is Sissel," she exclaimed. "We need to figure out exactly what happened between her and Inger. You heard Oaken. He knew things about Inger we didn't. There's got to be a piece of the story we're missing. And maybe whatever it is can help us understand Sissel and what she might want."

Elsa nodded. "It's not a bad idea," she agreed. "But how can we figure out what really happened? Everyone seems to remember it differently. And most of Arendelle doesn't remember anything at all."

"True. But it must have been written down at one point," Anna reminded her. "I mean, it had to be a big story, right? Two princesses visiting Arendelle, and one of them murdering the other? In fact, I bet it was front-page news."

Her sister's eyes widened. "Of course! The *Village Crown*. Their archives go back for years."

"Maybe we can start there," Anna said. "I mean, it's worth a try, right?"

"Absolutely. We should get back to Arendelle as quickly as possible." Elsa turned to Grand Pabbie. "Thank you for your help," she said. "We'll take it from here."

Grand Pabbie cleared his throat. "Your Majesties, I hope you find what you seek," he said. "And quickly, too." He glanced worriedly at Kristoff, who was wandering around aimlessly, happily chatting with rocks that appeared to be actual rocks—not trolls. "In the meantime, why don't you leave Kristoff with us? We can watch over him until you . . . resolve . . . the situation."

"What? Leave Kristoff?" Anna cried, horrified. Suddenly all her newfound confidence and excitement about solving the mystery seemed to shatter. They wanted her to leave her fiancé behind?

"He'll be safe from the draugr here," Elsa reminded her gently.

Anna bowed her head. She knew her sister was right. But still, the thought of leaving him . . .

"Okay. But you'll have to keep Sven, too," she blurted out. "Even if Kristoff doesn't remember him, those two are never apart."

Bulda placed a hand on her knee. "Of course! Sven is always welcome here. . . ."

Anna nodded, vacantly, her eyes locking on her fiancé, and her stomach did a somersault all over again. "Just give me a moment to say goodbye. I mean, so long for now," she corrected herself.

"Of course," said Elsa, her eyes filled with sympathy. "We'll give you some space."

As much as Anna wanted breathing room, she wasn't looking forward to this farewell. She made her way over to Kristoff and Sven, who were now at least chatting with an actual troll instead of a lifeless rock.

"So you say you're earning a crystal during this celebration?" Kristoff was saying. "What do these crystals do?"

Little Rock laughed. "Oh, Kristoff!" He saw Anna and smiled. "Hey, your bride is here." He then bounded off to find the others.

Kristoff did a double take at Anna. "My bride?" His cheeks reddened.

So did hers. "I'm not your bride," she said quickly. *Not yet, anyway,* she thought. "But I am someone who cares about you very much." She touched his cheeks, which were windburned and cold. "That's why I'm going to leave you and Sven here with Bulda for a few days. Bulda will take good care of you till I get back."

"Okay," Kristoff said happily. "And you're coming back because . . . ?"

Anna felt her heart squeeze so tightly that she lost her breath. But she would be brave. She would not let Kristoff see how scared she was for him and their kingdom. She would make things right. And then she'd never, *ever* let him tell another campfire story again.

Anna leaned in and kissed him on the lips. "Because I love you," she said, holding his face close. "And you love me, and we've got a whole future to plan when I get back and you start remembering things again." She stepped away, her heart hurting more than she thought was possible. Her voice was hoarse as she continued, "So stay safe till I do, okay?"

"Okay," said Kristoff. "Come along, Sven. Let's go find this Bulda lady." He paused, then turned to Anna. "Goodbye, Miss Bride!"

Anna ached as she watched him wander through the crowd of trolls without a care in the world. *He doesn't remember us*, she thought. *He doesn't remember me.* She wanted to cry, but now was when she needed to be strong. So instead, she squared her shoulders and watched from a growing distance as Bulda took his hands and within seconds was talking fast about some terrible-sounding soup that she swore would fix Kristoff and Sven right up.

Anna hoped Bulda was right, but she knew in her heart nothing would bring the love of her life back to her till this draugr business was finished once and for all.

Snow had started falling again as they stopped to pick up Olaf at Oaken's Trading Post and Sauna and then made their way back into the village later in the day. When they arrived in Arendelle, lights were flickering in every window, but it didn't appear as if anyone was working on the Polar Nights festivities. In fact, it was as if they didn't remember the celebration at all.

As they walked toward the newspaper office, they ran into Mattias, who was sitting beneath their parents' tribute statue, staring down at a photo of himself and Halima, shaking his head, looking puzzled.

"We're back," Anna told him. "How has everything been since we were gone?"

Mattias glanced up at the two of them, a blank look on his face. "Everything is fine," he said flatly. "Why wouldn't it be?"

Anna's chest tightened. "Uh, I don't know. Pirates off our shores? Crazy strong storms? Weird zombies lurking in the shadows?"

"I haven't heard any of that," Mattias said with a shrug; Anna's stomach plummeted. Mattias pushed the photo in his hands in their direction. "Do you happen to know who this is? She looks so familiar, but I can't place her."

"Someone special. I think you'll find her over there," Elsa said, helping him up from his seat and gently directing him toward Hudson's Hearth—the tavern owned by the love of his life, whom he currently didn't seem to remember. Mattias nodded vacantly, then started toward the building. But he seemed to forget where he was going before he was halfway there. Suddenly he began walking in the other direction, whistling tunelessly.

Elsa shot Anna a concerned look. "This isn't good,"

she said. "If Mattias has lost his memories, too, there's no one to look out for Arendelle."

"All the more reason we need to get to the bottom of Inger and Sissel's story fast," Anna declared, trying not to show how worried she was inside. Her people were counting on her. Kristoff was counting on her—whether he remembered it or not. She couldn't let any of them down.

And I won't, she told herself firmly. *One way or another, we're going to stop this draugr. We're going to make things right.*

"Come on," she said to Elsa. "Let's go find Wael."

"Oh, hello!" Wael said as he opened the door to the office of the *Village Crown,* which he lived above. Anna, Elsa, and Olaf filed in, taking in the smell of ink and warm paper that greeted them. "It's so nice to have company!"

Anna was startled. The office was a mess, and papers were everywhere. That was not like Wael.

"'Nice to have company'? This is new," Olaf mumbled. Wael was usually too busy to talk unless he was doing an interview, and when he was working, he was super serious.

"Wael, we were actually hoping to ask you some questions about the paper," Anna started right in.

Wael's face fell. "I'm afraid there is no new issue this week. I seem to have forgotten how to work my printing press . . . and I can't find my ink. Have you seen my pencil anywhere?"

Elsa reached up and pulled it out from where it was tucked behind Wael's ear.

"Oh!" Wael chuckled. "Silly me! So forgetful today."

Anna glanced at her sister. "That's what we were afraid of." It appeared, like everyone else, Wael would be no help. Any research would have to be done on their own.

"Wael," Elsa addressed him. "We're hoping to look at your archives. Where do you keep all the old issues of the paper?"

Wael brightened. "In the back room! I have all of them, dating back to the paper's first issue." He hurried ahead of them, dodging stacks of this week's forgotten issue. "The *Village Crown* has been around for . . . uh . . ."

"Sixty years," Olaf offered.

"Right!" Wael said, smiling again. "Nice to meet fans of our work." He opened the door to the back room, and Anna saw walls of bookshelves with papers stacked on them. "Take your time and look at anything you want," Wael said. "I'll be in the other room, um . . . working on something." He chuckled to himself and disappeared.

"Well," Elsa said as she went to the first bookshelf. "At least a forgetful Wael is a friendly Wael."

"Okay, let's divide and conquer," Anna said, heading to the second bookshelf. "We're looking for a story that ran about fifty years ago."

"That narrows it down," said Olaf, hopping up on a stool and tackling the third bookcase.

The search took a while, Anna's patience wearing thin as Wael whistled happily in the next room. Before long, the place looked like a hurricane had hit it, with stacks of papers now piled in disarray high on either side of them and scattered all over the floor. (Turned out, Olaf's version of researching was a bit . . . messy.) They'd found all sorts of interesting stories from years past: their parents' wedding announcement, the grand opening of Blodget's Bakery, the tragic story of Queen

Rita—King Runeard's wife and their grandmother—and her strange disappearance when their father was just a small child. But nothing about the Vesterland sisters.

"Ooh, here's a story about your birth, Anna!" Olaf announced excitedly, pushing a crumpled paper in her direction. Anna scanned the front page, then frowned.

"Uh, where?" she asked, confused.

"It's right there!" Olaf pointed to the bottom of the page. "Right under that really big article about 'Old Blue Eyes' the Pirate Queen threatening Arendelle's shores!"

"Of course it is," Anna grumbled, her eyes falling to the much smaller headline, ARENDELLE WELCOMES THEIR SECOND PRINCESS! Clearly the *Village Crown*'s obsession with pirates ran deep. . . .

"I think I found something!" Elsa shouted, jumping down from a top shelf with several papers in her arms. She dropped them on the table and pointed to the paper on top. "It's an article about the Vesterland sisters visiting Arendelle. And the timing is right." She laid out the newspaper on the table. Sure enough, there was a drawing of two girls—one with long hair tied up in complicated braids and one with a short bob—staring back at them. Elsa touched the newspaper. "That's them.

The same girls in Oaken's portrait." She pointed to the long-haired girl. "Inger," she said, then moved her hand to the girl with the bob. "And Sissel."

"I have to say, Sissel's a lot prettier as a real girl than a rotting zombie," Olaf observed. "I mean, not that looks matter. It's what's in your heart that counts."

Anna stared at the picture of Sissel. It was hard to believe the creature that had attacked them had once been this beautiful girl. She looked so happy, as if she hadn't had a care in the world. But then, so did Inger, who was smiling adoringly up at her sister in the picture, like she worshipped the ground Sissel walked on. One thing was for sure: they definitely didn't look like mortal enemies.

Elsa started reading the story aloud. "'The *Village Crown* is pleased to report that the princesses of Vesterland, known as the Vesterland sisters, are coming to Arendelle for an important meeting with King Runeard.'"

Anna frowned. "An important meeting? About what?"

"It doesn't say," Elsa told her, flipping ahead to another story. "Here's one about the accident, though."

The three of them leaned over the paper and read the article at the same time.

"It's just like everyone in the village has already been saying," Anna said, knowing she sounded disappointed. "Inger and Sissel had an argument, and Sissel drowned. Inger was charged with her murder, and Grandfather had her sent away on a prison ship to be banished. It went down at sea in a storm before it made it to its destination. There's nothing else to report."

"If Inger is dead, then what could Sissel be after by appearing now?" Elsa asked. "Not revenge, clearly."

"I don't know. But this isn't telling us anything new." She put the paper back down. "We need to find out more about the sisters themselves. Or what they were arguing about that was so bad it led to murder."

"Well, we won't find that here," Elsa said.

Anna nodded slowly, feeling discouraged. "And clearly no one in Arendelle remembers anything," she began. Then a thought came to her. "That's it! Why didn't I think of this before?"

"What?" Elsa asked, looking puzzled.

"We need to go to Vesterland!" Anna said, getting excited. "Maybe King Jonas and Mari know why Inger and Sissel were here in Arendelle or what they were arguing about. I mean, that's their home kingdom! If anyone would know, it would be them!"

"Great idea, Anna," Elsa agreed. "A visit to King Jonas could solve all our problems."

Anna smiled dreamily as she closed the book. *Solve all our problems. Get Kristoff back.* She suddenly felt hopeful. "Let's inform Mattias and leave first thing in the morning."

CHAPTER THIRTEEN

Elsa

ELSA USUALLY LOVED SLEEPING in her parents' bed. She knew it was impossible, but she swore it still smelled a little like Mother's perfume, which had always been so earthy, reminding her of the smoky, rich smells of the Enchanted Forest. She was grateful that Anna had let her keep the bedroom even though she didn't officially live there, but then, that was Anna, right? She always wanted to make her sister feel at home.

And Arendelle would always be a home to Elsa. Though once it had felt like a prison cell, she'd grown to love the castle, thanks to the help of the memories in Ahtohollan and the love of her sister. She still adored the outdoors, of course, where she could be one with nature and the spirits—where she could truly "let it go." But there was also something cozy and warm about being surrounded by four walls and the people you loved.

Truly she had the best of both worlds.

Except for the moment, of course, with the wind howling so loud it made it difficult to sleep. The air was dry and cold, and she could see the snow billowing on the castle ramparts. Another blizzard, blanketing the town in white. And this time it was not the fault of the Snow Queen.

It had taken hours to get all the livestock safely in their pens and the doors locked tight against the winds. Especially since half the town had forgotten how to make storm preparations for their animals. Or that they even had animals. The memory loss was getting worse, and she worried that someone was going to end up killed—because they forgot how hot a fire was, or the fact that they couldn't breathe underwater—if they didn't figure out a way to end this soon.

And then there was Kristoff. She'd been trying so hard to be brave for Anna's sake. But deep down she was terrified for the ice harvester who had stolen her sister's heart. As much as Kristoff could be rough around the edges, she'd grown to love him like a brother. Loved how good he was for, and to, her sister. Anna was independent, smart, and capable of taking care of herself, of course. But it was always nice to have someone to lean on every once in a while. Or simply share jokes with. What would Anna do if Kristoff's memory was gone for good?

Elsa tossed from side to side, but try as she might, sleep wouldn't come. The storm was too loud and there was too much on her mind. Grand Pabbie's words kept rolling in her head, over and over: *Day will forever be cast into night.*

This warning would have been difficult for anyone. But for Elsa, who had finally embraced the sun and its warm rays after a lifetime of living in her dark room, it felt especially cruel. Eternal night was worse than eternal winter. How could she live without the sun dappling the golden trees in the Enchanted Forest? Without the warmth of its rays on her cool skin?

She rubbed her eyes, giving up on sleep. Sitting up in bed, Elsa turned and lowered her feet to the floor, sliding them into fuzzy slippers. Maybe Anna was still up, too. Maybe they could slip down to the kitchen and heat up some warm milk to drink like they used to ask Olina to do when they were little. They could talk about their upcoming journey to Vesterland and work out the details. It wasn't going to be easy to get there if the storm didn't let up, especially since they'd left Sven and Kristoff's sleigh with the trolls. Elsa had fashioned an ice sled for the way down the mountain, but Anna had half frozen to death during the short journey, despite all the moss the trolls had laid down on the bench seat. They could go by horseback, but that seemed risky, too, especially after what had happened on the way back from Sorenson's. Still, it might be their only choice.

Rising to her feet, Elsa headed to the door, giving one last look at the storm outside. It seemed to have intensified even more, the wind battering at her window as if begging to come inside.

"Just give it a rest," she muttered, as if Sissel could hear her. "Go bug your sister if you're that mad. After all, she's the one who murdered you, not us!" Elsa knew she sounded grumpy, but she couldn't help it. Somehow, they'd gotten stuck in the middle of a fifty-year-old feud. As if their own problems weren't enough to deal with.

She slipped out the door and tiptoed down the hall.

Everything was silent and dark and kind of creepy, given her current mood. Elsa tried not to imagine the draugr hiding in the dark places. Watching, waiting for a chance to strike.

Suddenly, a shadow crossed over a portrait of her parents at the far wall. She froze in her tracks, breath caught in her throat. Then she let out a sigh of relief as she realized it was only Sassy, one of the castle cats, scurrying after a mouse. She leaned down and scooped up the calico in her arms, rejoicing in the feel of the cat's soft fur against her trembling fingers.

"Don't scare me like that," Elsa scolded gently, scratching the cat's ears. Sassy meowed and nuzzled her hand. She smiled. "Maybe you're the one who needs the warm . . ."

But the words died in her throat as her ears caught another noise coming from down the hall. She swallowed hard, straining to hear. Another cat? But no, this sounded more like moaning than a meow or a purr. She set Sassy down on the floor and crept forward, heart being wildly in her chest.

The sound came again. But no, not just a sound. It was a voice!

"Wrongggggggg . . . Issssss . . . WRONGGGGGGGG . . ."

Elsa froze, her pulse kicking up in alarm. Sissel! And she sounded close, too. She picked up the pace, running down the hall as fast as her slippered feet would take her.

"Anna!" she called out, not caring if she woke the whole castle. If the draugr did something to her sister . . . "Anna! Wake up!"

She whipped around the corner and almost slipped on the hallway rug. To her horror, Anna's door was wide open. Anna never slept with an open door—she claimed the early morning servants were too loud and would wake her up. What had pushed it open?

Or . . . who?

Elsa dashed into the room, then stopped dead in her tracks. Her eyes bulged from her head. There was Anna, sound asleep in her bed, her hair a rat's nest of tangles, a large splotch of drool sliding down her chin—and a monstrous draugr looming above her.

"No!" Elsa screamed. Without thinking, she raised her hands, shooting bolts of ice in the draugr's direction. The draugr screamed as a blast hit it square in the chest, knocking it backward. Elsa dashed forward, throwing herself on the bed between Anna and the creature.

"Leave Anna alone!" she cried. "She's not your evil sister Inger!"

The creature froze, cocking its head curiously. Had the name Inger registered somehow? Elsa hoped she hadn't accidentally made it angrier by bringing up her murderer.

Elsa's gaze shifted to Anna, still sound asleep. Fear gripped her heart with icy fingers. Had Sissel been trying to steal her sister's memories?

Had she succeeded?

The draugr made its move, dashing past Elsa and bolting for the door. For a moment, Elsa wasn't sure what to do. Should she stay with her sister to make sure she was all right? Or go after the creature? But then she knew what Anna would want her to do. She leapt off the bed and gave chase.

The draugr was quick, racing down the halls while Elsa struggled to keep up. Down the stairs, across the first great hall, toward the kitchen, passing a sleeping Olina in an old wooden chair and heading into the ice room in the back.

Elsa gasped. The draugr was headed toward the Earth Giant's Passage underneath the castle. But how did she know about that? Only Elsa and Anna—

Anna. The draugr had stolen the memory of the passageway from Anna. Of course!

Elsa dashed into the ice room. Sure enough, the three flagstones that covered the entrance to the secret passageway had been strewn across the room, revealing a gaping black hole dropping down into the earth. The draugr had to be down there somewhere. Hoping to escape with her sister's memories—and those of who knew how many others?

"Oh no you don't!" warned Elsa as she dove into the passageway, taking the stone steps two at a time, descending into darkness. In her haste, she hadn't thought to bring a lantern. She didn't love the idea of facing a draugr she couldn't see. She could hear it moaning in the not-so-far distance beyond, along with a spine-tingling scraping that sounded like claws against stone.

"Bruni?" she called out, hoping the Fire Spirit had followed when she left her room. "I could use some help here!"

A moment later, there was a flash of purple-hued light. She let out a breath of relief as the salamander leapt onto her shoulder.

"Thank you," she whispered. "You're a lifesaver."

Bruni gurgled and slurped her cheek with its tongue, which would have made Elsa laugh if she hadn't been so scared.

She drew in a shaky breath. Okay, time to find that draugr and confront it once and for all. She picked up the pace, heading down the tunnel as fast as she dared. Bruni's fire cast strange shadows on the rough stone walls as they went, making things extra creepy. Was the draugr lying around the next corner, waiting to pounce? Or was it attempting to make an escape? There was no way to tell for sure. Elsa knew the passageway eventually dead-ended at a waterfall that led out to a ledge overlooking Arendelle. Maybe she could corner it there and make it talk.

If it *could* talk . . .

Elsa turned the corner, stopping short as she came face to face with the draugr, silhouetted by the waterfall behind it. It looked even more sinister in the dim light, its shadow huge and monstrous against the stone wall. Elsa took a hesitant step backward as it moved toward her, gnashing its broken teeth.

Suddenly, Elsa felt light-headed. She swayed a little and Bruni chirped in alarm. Grabbing the wall, she righted herself, then put a hand to her forehead. She could feel something cold there against her skin.

Oh, no! Was Sissel trying to steal her memories, too? Right then and there?

No! She wouldn't let that happen. She shook her head, squaring her shoulders. Lifting her chin. "You leave my memories alone!" she cried.

She raised a hand and ice flew from her fingers, just missing the draugr. It moaned in what sounded like dismay, turning to flee, but there was nowhere left for it to go. The waterfall loomed behind it, and Elsa watched with a mixture of fear and fascination as the creature took a hesitant step backward. Moaning softly.

"Water," she whispered in realization. "You're afraid of water. . . ."

And of course it was. Sissel had been drowned by her own sister. Washed out to sea. Elsa realized this was her chance. She raised her hands, ice crackling at her fingertips. Then she released it, shooting the draugr straight on. It screamed as the ice spread across its rotting flesh, freezing it in place. The monster tried to thrash free, but Elsa was too quick, sending a second bolt of ice in its direction. The draugr wailed in anguish but was stuck fast.

Elsa let out a breath of relief. This wouldn't hold, but it would give her some time. Time to get some answers from this thing.

"Why are you doing this?" she demanded. "Why are you terrorizing our town? What did we do to you?"

The draugr moaned mournfully. *"Sissssssterrrrrrrrrr."*

"You mean Inger?" Elsa asked. "I know she drowned you, and that's pretty awful, but why are you stealing memories from the people of Arendelle?" She couldn't believe she was sympathizing with this creature. "We didn't have anything to do with that! Just leave Arendelle alone!"

The draugr thrashed again. This time Elsa saw cracks form in its icy prison. She wouldn't be able to hold it for much longer. She tried to shoot another blast of ice, but this time it wouldn't come out. Just like before in the woods, her powers were beginning to fizzle. More of the draugr's magic, she assumed.

Which meant she had to get out of there. Fast.

But then she'd miss her chance.

"If there is something you're trying to tell us, tell us!" Elsa cried. "Don't steal memories! Our people didn't push you in the river! It was your sister who hurt you, not them! Leave Arendelle and bring back the sun!"

The draugr roared now, looking more and more furious. The ice was cracking faster, and Elsa didn't know how long it would hold. As it turned out . . . not long at all. It shattered, and Elsa had to duck to avoid being stabbed by a flying razor-sharp shard. When she stood up again, the draugr was leaning over her with a terrible look on its misshapen face.

"*Wrongggggggggg.*

"*Sissssssterrrrrrrrr.*

"*You're . . . wronggggggg!*"

The draugr raised its hands. To Elsa's horror, she saw ice crackling from Sissel's rotted fingers. *Oh, no!* She threw herself to the side, but it did no good. Sissel shot a sheet of ice straight at her, locking her against the wall.

Her ice. Reflected back at her from the draugr.

Elsa struggled to free herself, but to no avail. The draugr gave her one last look, then bolted toward the waterfall, freezing it in place. It whacked the ice with its fist, shattering it into a million pieces. It glanced back at Elsa once more, then leapt off the cliff, disappearing from view.

A moment later, Elsa's icy prison broke around her, too, freeing her from its grasp. She ran to the cliff's edge and looked down. But she saw no sign of the draugr.

It was gone.

Except . . .

She frowned as she reached down to the rocky ground, picking up a small object in her hand. A bracelet. She gasped. It wasn't just any bracelet, but the one she'd given Anna on her birthday a few years back.

A present to her sister. To show how much she was loved. Elsa had even had the silver bangle inscribed with a message—*A Sister's Love.*

A sister's love . . .

Sissel's words suddenly seemed to echo in Elsa's ears. *Wronggggggggg.*

You're . . . wrongggggggg!

Elsa's mind flashed back to the memory she'd seen in Ahtohallan. Sissel being swept away by the river. Inger crying on the shore. Then she thought of Oaken's story of his father playing with the two princesses. He'd claimed they were close. Anna had been right—there was more to the story, and if they didn't figure out what it was, Arendelle was going to suffer because of it.

CHAPTER FOURTEEN

Anna

ANNA AWOKE WITH A START and found Elsa standing over her, worry lines etched on her face. "What happened?" asked Anna as she sat up fast. "Is it the draugr?"

Elsa's whole body seemed to collapse. "You remember the draugr?" Anna was surprised to hear a tremble in her voice. "You remember . . . me?"

Anna blinked. "Of course I remember you, silly! Best sister in the world? Amazing magical ice powers? Really good taste in chocolate?"

Elsa sat on the edge of the bed and pulled Anna into

a tight embrace. Anna could feel her sister shaking. She suddenly felt very cold.

"Hey, Elsa . . . what's wrong?" she whispered.

"I thought . . . I was sure . . . I didn't know if I got to you in time," Elsa said, sounding unsure and frightened, which was not a side of her Anna was used to seeing anymore. Elsa pulled away from their embrace, locking eyes with her. "I caught the draugr in your room."

"What?" Anna inhaled sharply, holding her chest. *No.* Sissel had been here? In her room? She shuddered at the idea of the draugr standing over her. Stealing memories! She closed her eyes and tried to think of all the things she loved—Elsa, Kristoff, Olaf, Sven, her kingdom, her parents—and could see memories of each of them form in her mind. "I don't think she got anything," she said, opening her eyes again.

"Good." Elsa sounded relieved.

"But how can I be sure?" Anna smoothed her hair, which, as usual, was sticking up in a million directions after a restless night's sleep. A restless night's sleep that evidently included an encounter with a draugr. She swallowed hard, feeling nervous again. "Quick! Ask me something! Anything! I want to make sure I remember it all."

Elsa thought for a moment. "Favorite food?"

Anna rolled her eyes. "Sandwiches. I mean something harder! Something specific."

"Okay." Elsa pursed her lips. "You're planning a big celebration this week. What is it?"

"*Elsa,*" Anna groaned. "I clearly remember the Polar Nights festival! It's like the biggest thing ever!"

"I know! But this is good. You're remembering the important things," Elsa said, looking relieved.

"Give me something challenging," Anna demanded, making fists like she was ready to fight.

"Biggest mistake of your life?"

"Hans, obviously!" Anna moaned and threw herself back on the pillows. "You're not doing this right. Ask me something that's really specific, like what I had for breakfast yesterday." She sat up, then grinned. "Porridge!" she said triumphantly. "Ha!"

Elsa nodded. "Okay, and after the porridge, we went . . ."

"Easy, we went . . ." Anna paled. Unlike Elsa's previous

questions, this time the answer didn't immediately come to her. "We went . . ." She racked her brain trying to remember where they'd been, but it was as if her mind post-breakfast had been wiped clean. Anna felt slightly ill. "I don't know."

Elsa placed a hand over Anna's. "We went to see Grand Pabbie and the trolls. And Kristoff . . ."

Suddenly everything came rushing back at Anna. She closed her eyes, a sick feeling welling in her stomach. "Kristoff," she whispered. "He doesn't . . . remember me." Her voice got caught in her throat. She could feel her heart beat so fast it might break. "He doesn't remember our engagement. Or even our Choco-versary . . ."

"But he will," responded Elsa, voice firm. "He will remember all those things, just as you do. Once we figure out Sissel's story, we can end this."

Anna nodded, shifting positions on the bed. Her hand brushed against something nestled in the quilt. She reached down and pulled out a tarnished necklace with a silver locket attached to it. "What's this?"

"I don't know," Elsa said. "It's not yours?"

"Give me some credit. I take better care of my

jewelry than this." Anna examined the tarnished chain and pulled at the clasp. The heart-shaped locket popped open, revealing two faded portraits. One was of a girl with long braids, and the other was of a girl with a short bob. Anna gasped. "Are those . . . ?"

Elsa stared down at the locket with wonder in her eyes. "Inger and Sissel? I think so. Though the pictures are so warped! It's like they've been underwater for years."

The two sisters looked up at each other. Underwater. Like Sissel.

Elsa's eyes widened. "Oh my gosh. I almost forgot!" She reached into her robe pocket, then placed a familiar bracelet in Anna's hand. "When I chased Sissel away from your room, she dropped this. She must have taken it from your jewelry box!"

Anna flipped it over and read the inscription Elsa had etched inside. A SISTER'S LOVE. "So she left me her locket and took my bracelet. What is she trying to tell us?"

"I don't know." Elsa said. "But it has to mean something. She kept moaning something that sounded like 'You're wrong.' "

"As if we don't already know that," Anna groaned. "It would be a lot more helpful if she could just tell us what's right."

"Well, that's what we're working on today," Elsa said firmly, reaching for Anna to pull her out of bed. She paused, looking at her questioningly. "Do you remember where we're going?"

Anna thought for a moment. "We're going to Vesterland!" she said triumphantly. "To talk to King Jonas and Princess Mari!" *Take that, Sissel!* She bounced out of bed. "So what are we waiting here for? Let's go solve this Sissel and Inger mystery!"

The journey to Vesterland took longer than it should have. The raging storm was only getting worse, and it seemed to follow them the entire way, with the snow coming down so hard it was difficult for Anna and Havski to see even with the Water Nokk running ahead to clear the path. The skies, if possible, had only grown more sinister, with lightning continuing to flash through the clouds and low rumbles of thunder sounding like avalanches. If not for Bruni lighting the way, it would have been pitch dark. At one point, Anna wasn't even sure they were going to make it—would they have to turn back?—but at last she glimpsed the familiar sight of Vesterland's castle courtyard, with its massive fountain standing out and marking the path ahead.

The sisters hopped off their horses, with Anna tying Havski up in the royal barn while the Water Nokk spirited itself away; then they trudged through the mounting snow to reach the castle itself. There wasn't a soul to be seen outside. Elsa grabbed the large knocker and rapped it against the door, her fingers frozen to the bones.

The doors opened slowly, revealing two servants flanked by half a dozen guards, their swords aimed right at Anna and Elsa's chests.

Anna gasped. *What on earth?*

Elsa reacted instantly, raising her hands to use her powers. Anna leapt in front of her, grabbing her sister's hands and lowering them before there was an international incident. Then she turned to the guards, hoping she looked brave, but not threatening.

"I'm Queen Anna of Arendelle," she said. "And this is my sister, Elsa. We're here to see King Jonas and Princess Mari. . . ."

The guards exchanged glances. But they didn't lower their weapons. What was going on here?

"Sorry we didn't send word we were coming, but it's urgent," Anna tried again. "If you could just—"

"Anna? Elsa?" Mari came racing down the stairs behind the guards and addressed the men. "You can put down your swords. These are my friends." The guards reluctantly lowered their weapons. Mari gave an apologetic shrug. "I'm so sorry. We're on high alert here."

Because of the draugr, Anna thought. Sissel must have come to Vesterland, too. "That's why we're here," she told her friend, wrapping her in a hug.

"Did you bring Olaf?" Mari asked, turning to hug Elsa as well. Mari was a big fan of the snowman's hugs. And he was a big fan of her cookies.

"No. He's back in Arendelle," Elsa said.

"We kind of left him in charge," Anna added sheepishly. "It's a long story." The snowman had wanted to come with them, but they'd insisted he stay home. After all, they needed *someone* not affected by Sissel's powers to keep an eye on the kingdom while they were gone. And, for better or worse for the kingdom, with Mattias now affected too, Olaf was the only one left. Anna tried hard not to think about that. "We have to talk to your father at once. Is he here?"

"Of course!" Mari said, grabbing their arms and leading the way to the king's chambers. "We were headed to Arendelle to join you at the Polar Nights festival, but with everything going on, we weren't sure if it was safe to go."

"Because of the weather?" Elsa asked.

"Because of the draugr?" Anna guessed at the same time.

Mari looked at them both in surprise as she knocked on her father's chamber door. "No! Because of the pirates."

King Jonas's doors opened and the king appeared before they could clear things up.

"Queen Anna," King Jonas said, reaching out to shake her hand. "Queen Elsa. I'm glad you're both here. Are you all right? We feared the worst when we heard the pirates were headed to Arendelle's port."

Anna stared at him. It was funny; with all that had been going on, she had almost forgotten their potential pirate problem. It seemed so inconsequential when compared to everything else. Still, it would definitely need to be addressed at some point—hopefully after they cleared everything else up.

"We tried sending messengers to see if you needed help," King Jonas added. "But they all came back acting confused, as if they'd forgotten why they were headed to Arendelle in the first place." He scratched his head. "So strange."

"Also, the storms have been really bad," Mari added. "Which has put everyone on edge."

Anna nodded and took a deep breath before addressing the king and Mari. "That's part of the reason why we're here. Your messengers' memory loss? It's our fault," she admitted. "It seems we've accidentally unleashed a draugr, and it's causing all kinds of havoc—including memory loss and these terrible storms. In fact, probably the only thing we can't blame on it is the pirates."

"So you came to warn us?" Mari asked.

"Well, yes," Elsa said hesitantly. "But also because we think you might be the only ones who can help us stop it."

"Really?" Mari raised her eyebrows. "How can we help?"

"We're pretty sure our not-so-friendly draugr was once Sissel, princess of Vesterland," Anna explained. "Heir to the throne before your father." She quickly explained the story as she knew it. Then she turned to King Jonas. "There's so much hearsay about the Vesterland sisters, but we're trying to learn the true story. We were hoping you might have known them back when you were all kids. You would be related, right?"

King Jonas nodded. "They were my cousins. And I did know of them. I think I even met them once or twice when I was really young. But after their parents died, they kind of kept to themselves in the castle. It was tragic, really. But at least they had each other." He shifted. "Well, until, you know . . ."

Anna and Elsa exchanged looks, and Anna knew what her sister was thinking. In so many ways the lives of the Vesterland sisters mirrored their own. Who would have ruled Arendelle if they'd suffered the same fate? (Maybe Hans? Anna decided she would definitely have come back as a draugr to tear things up if that were the case!)

"It's the 'you know' part we're trying to learn more about," Elsa explained. "We want to find out what really happened on their trip to Arendelle right before Sissel drowned. Everyone back home seems to remember the sisters' visit differently. But no one seems to know exactly why they were visiting in the first place."

"Oh, I can answer that," King Jonas said as he sat up straighter. "I believe they were there to meet with King Runeard about his dam project. It was in the beginning stages then, and Runeard was working to get all the neighboring kingdoms to help fund the endeavor."

"Of course." Anna looked at her sister in realization. "The dam was built almost fifty years ago. The timing totally makes sense."

"Was Sissel in favor of the project?" Elsa asked, a hint of distaste in her voice. And for good reason, too. As they now knew, the dam their grandfather had been planning ended up being disastrous to the environment, cutting off the water supply for the Northuldra and drying up their lands. It was only recently, after Anna finally destroyed the dam with the help of the Earth Giants, that the land had begun to recover and things had gotten back to normal.

King Jonas scratched his beard. "I can't say for certain, but if she wasn't, I couldn't imagine her standing up to King Runeard about it. From what I understand, she was pretty shy. It was her sister, Inger, who was the fighter in the family." He seemed to consider this for a moment. "Hmm. Maybe that's why she took Inger along with her on that trip to Arendelle?"

"Speaking of fighting, do you know if they got along?" Anna pressed. "Some say they were rivals and others say they loved each other. It's hard to get a straight story."

King Jonas chuckled and looked at Mari. "Sounds like typical siblings to me. Don't all brothers and sisters get along sometimes and fight like dogs at others?"

Anna and Elsa looked at one another and mumbled some variation of "yes."

King Jonas snapped his fingers. "You know who you should talk to about them? The Figels. They were their castle stewards who looked after them. They're retired now, but they practically raised the girls when they were younger."

"The Figels! Yes! We'd love to talk to them," Anna said, excitement welling inside of her. This was exactly what they needed: people who had actually known the sisters personally.

"I can take you to them," Mari said. "They live

right in the village. You'll love them!" She paused, then grinned. "Just . . . don't eat anything they try to serve you. Trust me, you'll thank me later."

The Figels' modest home was literally right outside the castle gates. Even better: someone answered on the first knock. The strong smell of garlic, onions, and cooked fish met them at the door.

"Oh my," Elsa whispered, inhaling sharply.

"Hello there, Mari!" said a tall woman with salt-and-pepper hair. She was dressed in a bright orange apron that covered an even brighter blue dress. "You're just in time! Olga and I were just trying out a new stew recipe."

Mari looked at Anna out of the corner of her eye. "Oh . . . I couldn't impose. I just wanted to stop by to introduce you to my friends."

"Nonsense!" said the woman, smiling at Anna. "We love company! I'm Helga. I'll tell my wife to set three more plates." She grabbed Mari's hand and yanked her inside. "OLGA! MARI IS HERE!"

The home was dark with the curtains drawn, but

tidy, with lots of knits and piles of socks everywhere. The smell of food was even stronger inside the house. Anna's eyes started to water. "That's so kind of you, but we actually just ate." Her stomach grumbled in response. Helga laughed.

"Looks like you've got room," she said, pulling out a chair for Anna. Elsa and Mari grabbed their own. "OLGA! EXTRA PLATES! She's a little hard of hearing these days," Helga told the group.

"I'm coming! I'm coming!" Olga came around the corner balancing three plates of steaming hot food in her arms. Her white hair was pulled up into a messy bun, and she was wearing a similar orange apron, which was splattered with all kinds of food. She saw the company waiting and smiled. "Hello, dears! What a nice surprise. So glad you can stay for lunch." She plunked down plates in front of the girls, and Anna could have sworn she smelled cloudberries in the dark brown soup.

She picked up her spoon warily. "Oh . . . how . . . nice. What is this?"

"*Lapskaus*," Helga told them. "We didn't have all the ingredients for Olga's mom's recipe, so we just winged it."

"We do that a lot," Olga told Anna. "We use whatever we have on hand, and it usually turns out okay."

"Usually," Helga seconded. "You should stay for dessert. We're making *tilslørte bondepiker*. It's delicious if you like apples."

"We're out of apples," Olga reminded her. "But we could try making it with onions! We have extra."

"Ooh, good idea!" Helga clapped her hands.

Anna's stomach turned at the thought of an onion-centric dessert. "We don't want to keep you from baking," Anna said quickly. "We were just hoping to talk to you about the Vesterland sisters. Mari mentioned you were their stewards."

"These are my friends, Anna and Elsa, the queens of Arendelle," Mari explained. "I told them you knew the girls well."

Helga's eyes lit up. "Oh! We haven't talked about them in a long time."

Olga hurried back into the room with two more plates for her and Helga. "We looked after them after their parents were gone, and we grew very close."

"I can imagine," Anna said softly. "Elsa and I are really close with our castle stewards, too." She thought of Kai and Gerda and her heart lurched. At the moment, they couldn't even remember who the girls were.

"That's lovely," Helga said. "We loved working for the family. Inger and Sissel were two peas in a pod, tighter than two sisters ever could be."

Olga's eyes locked on Anna. Her jaw dropped. "That locket you're wearing!" Her eyes narrowed suspiciously. "Where did you get that?"

"Um, it's a long story," Anna stammered.

"You recognize the locket?" Elsa pressed curiously.

"Recognize it! Of course I recognize it! I gave those lockets to the girls the year their parents died. So they'd remember they weren't alone. They'd always have each other." Olga sank into the chair, her eyes misting. "Inger lost hers immediately, of course. Silly girl. But she always got away with mishaps like that—she had these bright blue eyes that were—"

"Magnetic!" Helga finished. "Such an extraordinary color. And Sissel . . . she was always so into her appearance. She never took her necklace off. She told me it was her favorite piece of jewelry—and let me tell you, those two girls had their options when it came to jewels."

She hobbled up to Anna, palming the locket and

popping it open. She beckoned her wife to come over, all talk of stew thankfully forgotten.

"That's our girls," Helga said sadly. "I mean, they weren't ours, but they . . ."

"They felt like family," Olga finished. "Inger always acted like the older one—a tad bossy, as I told her, with Sissel as quiet as a mouse. But"—Olga shrugged—"Sissel was older, and it was her duty to take the throne, so Inger helped her best she could."

Anna snuck a glance at Elsa. Some of the similarities really were uncanny, personality-wise.

"Do you remember Inger ever talking about wanting to be queen?" Elsa asked.

Helga stirred a spoon in the stew in front of her. "I don't know about that. Inger was a naturalist—very concerned with the cutting down of trees and polluting water. She cared a lot about preserving Vesterland's waters, wildlife, and nature. Sissel, however, was more concerned with protecting alliances. She was a woman of the people."

That's what Oaken had said. Anna glanced at Elsa. A picture of the girls was becoming clearer. "Hmm. Sounds like they might have been divided on the dam project, then. I mean, if Inger realized its impact on the environment . . ."

Elsa's eyes widened in realization. "Do you think that's what they were fighting about, then? The dam project? I mean, it happened in Arendelle, right after they met with King Runeard."

Anna pursed her lips. "Maybe . . . but a fight that led to murder?" She looked up at Olga and Helga. It was time to just acknowledge the elephant in the room. "Do you think Inger murdered Sissel?"

Olga dropped her spoon in her stew. "Definitely not. I know what people say about the matter, but I can't believe it. I won't! Having known Inger, she would never . . ." She trailed off, unable to go on. Helga put her arm around her, producing a handkerchief from her pocket and giving it to her. Olga blew her nose loudly.

"We don't mean to bring up such a sad memory," Elsa said quietly. "We're just trying to figure out what really happened that day. If there's more to the story."

Helga nodded. "We've long wondered, too, but we've made our peace with it. We just try to remember the girls the way they were."

Anna's shoulders drooped. *Another dead end.*

"And honor their memory as best we can," Olga added, sighing deeply. "By bringing people to visit the memorial we built them in Arendelle."

Anna stopped twirling her spoon. "Memorial? What memorial?"

"After the incident, we traveled to Arendelle to try to find out what we could. We had someone take us to the spot where it happened—where Sissel . . ." Helga choked up. "We made a small memorial to both girls. Over the years it has been visited by many who loved them as we did."

Olga smiled proudly at her wife. "Helga carved a wooden statue of the girls that we brought there in our wagon. We planted wildflowers around it. They were Sissel's favorite."

Anna's heart started beating with excitement. A memorial. But more importantly, a memorial set up in the exact spot Sissel drowned. If they could get there, perhaps Elsa could use her powers to pull up a memory. And they could learn what had truly happened on that day.

This might prove to be their best lead yet.

"How would we find this memorial?" Elsa asked, her

voice catching. Her sister clearly had the same thoughts she did.

"We'll give you a map," Olga said. "We made them to share with others who wanted to make the pilgrimage to pay their respects. HELGA! Give the girls a map!"

"Stop yelling!" Helga chided her.

"I'm not yelling," Olga insisted and looked at Anna. "She's a bit hard of hearing."

Helga went to a curio cabinet and pulled open a bottom drawer, then produced a piece of parchment, which she handed to Elsa. On it was a drawing of Arendelle's rivers with an X next to one near the village. She pointed to it.

"Here you go. The very place where it all happened, fifty years ago."

Anna looked up at Elsa. "I think we've got our next clue."

CHAPTER FIFTEEN

Elsa

HELGA'S MAP, it turned out, wasn't exactly pinpoint accurate. In fact, they got lost in the dark woods three times before finally stumbling their way to the small, crude wooden statue honoring the two Vesterland princesses plopped down on a stone pedestal at a bend in the river. Elsa pointed to it with a cheer and Anna let out a sigh of relief, dropping off Havski and rushing over to it. She placed her hands on her hips, examining the carved wood.

"You know, maybe Sissel just wants a new memorial," she remarked, poking at the spot where Sissel's arm should have been. It had clearly broken off at some point over the years, and some of the wood was rotted clear through. "I mean, this one's kind of falling apart."

"Imagine if it were that simple." Elsa smiled as she slipped off the Water Nokk and stepped up to Anna. She squinted at the wooden memorial, which had clearly seen better days. She supposed fifty years of exposure to the elements would do that to any piece of wood. Still, the lettering at the bottom was clear enough to read.

BELOVED PRINCESSES. MAY YOU REST IN PEACE.

Hopefully they could make that happen—and soon, too.

"This is definitely the same spot I saw in my vision," Elsa mused, her eyes rising to the rapidly flowing water. "I remember that boulder just offshore. And that tree is much larger now, but it was definitely there," she added, pointing to a large oak with branches that hung over the river. She nodded. "Yes, this is definitely the spot where Sissel drowned."

"But did Inger do it?" Anna asked. "That's the question we need answered. And if she did—why? Everything we've learned about the sisters so far makes it seem like they were close. That they loved each other."

"Right. I mean, sure, they disagreed on a few things, but so what?" Elsa asked. "I mean, we disagree all the time."

"Usually about you putting yourself in danger," Anna pointed out.

Elsa snorted. She turned back to the memorial. "In my Ahtohallan vision, I saw Sissel struggling in the water. But we need to go back further. To hear what they were fighting about and what happened. That's the only way to know for sure."

She turned to the river. It was rushing past them pretty hard, tossing around large chunks of ice in the current. Very unlike the slow, serene section they were familiar with that ran by Arendelle's town center. Elsa guessed there might be a glacier nearby, feeding the river with melted snow. Even a good swimmer would have a tough time keeping their head above water there.

She dropped her hand into the river and felt the current through her fingers.

"Do you sense anything?" Anna asked eagerly. Elsa shook her head.

"Just freezing cold water," she replied, frowning. She closed her eyes, thinking of Sissel and Inger. Trying to imagine them on this shore. Arguing. What were they arguing about?

But nothing came to her.

It was then that she realized the problem. Water had memory. But this particular current wasn't the same water that had been here when Sissel had drowned. River water was constantly moving, always changing. If Elsa were in Ahtohallan, maybe she could manage to pull something up with the help of the spirit of memories. But here—she was on her own, and she wasn't sure it was going to work.

Elsa slumped onto the riverbank, feeling discouraged. What good were her powers if she couldn't use them to help anyone? Had this all been a dead end? Frustration began to rise inside of her. She squeezed her hands into fists.

"Hey! Elsa! Relax." She felt Anna by her side, putting her arms around her. "It's okay."

"It's not okay!" Elsa snapped. "I need to figure this out!" She squirmed free of Anna's grasp and dunked her hands in the freezing cold water again. Maybe if she could go deeper, she could find something. She squeezed her eyes shut. Trying, trying.

SPLASH!

Elsa screamed as she lost her balance, tumbling headfirst into the icy river. She thrashed around, trying to lodge her feet against the slippery stones, while choking on a mouthful of dirty water. The current was strong, dragging her downstream fast.

"Anna!" she cried, trying to use her magic to freeze the rushing water. But nothing happened. It was as if she were wearing gloves, even though she wasn't. She'd probably drained her powers reaching so deep, and now they were fizzling out again.

Oh, no. No, no, no!

"Anna! Help!" she cried again, knowing she sounded scared. Desperate. She fought to keep her head above water, to suck in air in the moments she could. But instead, she was gulping river water too fast, choking and sputtering as she tried again to find the river's bottom. But it was deep here and her feet only kicked uselessly as the current dragged her further down. Her body began to weaken. The riverbank seemed miles away.

"Elsa! I've got you!"

Suddenly, she felt strong arms grab her, dragging her to the shore. Anna heaved her onto dry land, then rolled her over, slapping her hard on the back until she hacked up all the dirty water. Elsa's heart pumped madly in her chest as she sucked in breath after breath of clean air.

"Are you okay?" Anna's voice sounded very concerned. "Elsa! Talk to me!"

She struggled to sit up. "I think so." She swallowed hard, trying to stop her body from shaking in a mixture of terror and cold. "I just leaned in too far."

"Yeah, I saw." Anna pursed her lips together. "You scared me half to death. I thought . . ." She trailed off, unable to continue. But Elsa knew exactly what she'd been thinking. That she'd almost shared Sissel's fate.

Elsa wrung out her white dress, staring at the river ruefully. "I guess now I understand how Sissel drowned," she said. "That current is rough."

"Lucky for you, you have a strong sister." Anna gathered up a small pile of wood and leaves. "Bruni?" she called out to the Fire Spirit when she was finished. "Want to help warm up your girl?"

The spirit leapt onto the small pile, easily igniting it with its flames. Soon they had a small fire giving off a nice hot glow. Elsa sighed gratefully, warming her hands. Her heart, however, was still beating very fast.

"So much for that plan," she said sorrowfully, giving the river an annoyed look. She hugged her chest. "Sorry I dragged you all the way out here," she said. "It was probably a dumb idea. I just thought . . . I mean, I remember pulling the memory from our parents' ship. But that water had been there for years—so the memories were still there, inside of it. This water is all new. There's nothing to pull from it. I'm sorry, Anna. I really wanted to figure out Sissel's story so we could end this." Her voice broke.

"Water has memory," Anna whispered thoughtfully.

"Yes. I just said that. But—"

"But the water here isn't the same. You need something that might have remnants of water from back then, right?"

"Right. But that's impossible. It was fifty years ago."

"Maybe not."

Elsa cocked her head in question. Anna lifted Sissel's locket from around her neck and held it out to her sister.

"Remember how the portraits seemed warped?" she

said. "Like they'd been underwater? Maybe they still have a bit of it in them."

"Anna! You're a genius!" Elsa plucked the locket from her sister's fingers, palming it in her hands. "The Figels told us Sissel never went anywhere without her locket. Which meant she must have been wearing it when she drowned." Her breath caught in her throat as hope surged through her. She tried to tell herself not to get too excited, but she couldn't help it.

She wrapped her fingers around the locket. Then she closed her eyes, searching deep for her powers. For a moment, she felt nothing and worried they had fizzled again. But then, slowly, the familiar feeling began to rise inside of her.

"It's working! Elsa, it's working!"

Elsa's eyes flew open. Sure enough, a small mist seemed to be rising from her closed hand. She released her fingers, opening them up one by one. The mist was twining out from the locket.

And suddenly they could see it perfectly. Two girls. One with long hair tied up in complicated braids. The other with a short bob.

"Inger and Sissel," Elsa breathed. Anna looked as

mesmerized as she felt. Even more so when the voices began to rise in the air.

"Inger, you need to stop arguing with him! It's not going to work."

"But, Sissel, we have to try! He's already started clearing land. If he builds that dam, it's going to destroy the Enchanted Forest and all the Northuldra's territory. It'll be an environmental disaster."

Elsa gasped. So they *had* been fighting about the dam that day! And Inger definitely wasn't in favor of it.

"Look, I understand. I really do," Sissel broke in. "But what are we going to do? King Runeard is never going to listen to us. And if we try to fight him on this, he's going to punish Vesterland. Our actual people. I mean, I care about reindeer and bunnies and all that, too, but I also care about our citizens. As their future queen, I need to protect them. Arendelle controls the port—all the food and supplies and medicine coming in from other kingdoms. Without that, we will suffer greatly."

"We will also suffer if all the animals die or migrate further north," Inger argued. "What are we going to hunt for food? He has to know the greater impacts his dam will have on our lands."

Sissel sighed. "He already knows. He just doesn't care."

"You have to make him care! That's what a queen would do!"

The sisters stared at one another, clearly at a standoff. Elsa glanced over at Anna, who was watching the scene with horrified eyes.

"Yeah, well, maybe *you* should be queen, then!" Sissel shot back. "If you're such an expert and all!"

"You know I don't want that," Inger protested, sounding hurt. "And you know I think you'll be an amazing queen. You're already an amazing sister. I'm just trying to help. Don't shut me out. Please!"

For a moment, Sissel just bristled. Then her shoulders began to slump. She sighed deeply, then gave her sister an apologetic look. "I'm sorry. I didn't mean that. I love you; you know that."

"And I love you." Inger reached for Sissel's hand. "We'll figure this out. One way or another."

Elsa watched, entranced, as the two sisters embraced on the side of the river. No longer fighting with one another, just hugging each other tightly. Just like she and Anna did after they argued.

"So it's true. Inger didn't want to be queen. She was just trying to help Sissel," Anna whispered, also looking on in awe. "She loved her sister."

"Then what happened between them that could have led to Sissel's death?" Elsa asked. "I don't get it."

"Just keep watching!" Anna urged. "There's got to be more."

But the vision was already fading. The magic drained from her fingers. Elsa gritted her teeth, trying to keep it going, but she could feel it falling away. The mist began to sputter from the necklace. The vision began to dim. She squeezed her eyes shut, straining. Feeling the ice crackle on her skin. No! After all this, she couldn't lose it now. She just couldn't!

"Elsa, look!"

Elsa's eyes shot open. Her mouth gaped, realizing they were no longer alone. Standing by the memorial statue, seeming to have come out of nowhere, was the draugr itself. Where had it come from? Had it followed them here?

This was not good. Not good at all.

"Anna, back away slowly. Don't make any sudden moves. I'll distract it and then find you later," Elsa whispered to her sister, her mind racing with a plan. Ice hadn't stopped the draugr last time. But maybe it could slow the creature down enough for them to get away.

She glanced at Anna, who hadn't moved. "What are you waiting for?" she cried, fear pounding in her heart. "Go!"

But Anna didn't go. Instead, she stepped between her sister and the draugr.

"What are you doing?" Elsa choked out, horrified. Her eyes locked onto the draugr, waiting for it to strike. Anna was too close. Far too close. It would only take one swipe of the creature's claws, and . . . "Anna, it's going to attack you!"

Or worse . . .

"No," Anna said firmly, keeping her eyes glued to it. "I think if it was, it would have done it already. I think it wants us here. I think it has something to show us. The draugr was the one who left us the locket," she reminded Elsa. "Maybe it hoped you could pull something from it. In fact, maybe that's why it's been haunting us all along. Because you're the only one with the power to see into the past. To discover the true story behind the sisters."

"*Sisssssster . . .*" the creature moaned, its eyes seemingly aflame when saying the word. "*Sisssssster. Minnnnne.*"

The draugr raised a rotted finger, pointing it toward the locket in Elsa's hand. For a moment, nothing happened. Then, suddenly, the sputtering stream of mist began to thicken, get stronger.

"Yes!" Anna cried out in excitement. "Yes!"

Elsa watched in amazement as more mist began to spill from the necklace, onto the riverbank, rebuilding the vision they'd been watching before. Slowly, with their combined magic, the vision grew more solid, real. As if the two girls were standing right in front of them.

"Now, let's see what *really* happened that day," Anna declared, her voice high-pitched with excitement.

Biting her lower lip, Elsa turned back to the scene playing out in front of them, concentrating hard to keep the magic flowing. Inger and Sissel were stepping out of their embrace, smiling at each other.

"I'm sorry," Inger said. "I don't want to fight with you."

"No, I'm sorry!" Sissel exclaimed. "You are right.

I've been a coward, not wanting to face Runeard. He scares me. But not as much as the idea of our lands being destroyed. Our people deserve better."

"So you're going to talk to him?" Inger asked, her voice rising in hope.

"Yes. We'll go back to Arendelle together, and I'll request another audience. I'm going to tell him Vesterland will not contribute to this project."

"And without our funding, he'll never get it off the ground!" Inger crowed. "Take that, Runeard." She raised a fist triumphantly, swinging her arm in the air as if punching their grandfather in the nose. Elsa started to laugh. She liked this girl!

But the laughter died in her throat as a noise rose in her ears. The roar of approaching water.

"A flash flood," Elsa gasped. "There was a flash flood."

No sooner had she said the words than it came into view. Rushing water racing down the river at top speed. Sissel screamed in horror. She leapt backward.

"Inger!" she cried. Her sister was right in the path of the water.

Inger's face turned white, but she didn't move. It was as if she was frozen by fear.

"Inger!" Sissel tried again. Her voice was full of panic. She dove for her sister, throwing herself at her, knocking her out of the water's path. But her foot caught on a root, and she tripped, falling into the water.

"Sissel!" Inger screamed. "No!"

Inger scrambled to her feet, dashing to the riverbank. Sissel was already far away, thrashing in the water just as Elsa had been doing moments before. With the water rougher because of the flood, waves rose over the shore, forcing Inger to stumble backward and further away.

"Inger!" Sissel cried. "Help me, Inger!" She tried to grab hold of a fallen log, then some outstretched branches—anything to stop from being pulled away. Meanwhile, Inger ran alongside the shore, screaming for help.

Elsa glanced at Anna, then started to run down the river, following the vision. Suddenly, she stopped short, her eyes bulging from her head as she realized what Sissel was headed for.

A giant waterfall.

"Look out, Sissel!" Inger cried, her face streaming with tears as she ran helplessly along the shore. "Look out!"

Sissel glanced behind her, her jaw dropping as she realized what was coming. She lunged for the shore again, this time managing to grab on to a small branch. She struggled to use it as a rope to pull herself to shore. But the current was too strong and the branch began to crack.

At that moment the vision froze, crystallizing into solid ice. Elsa frowned, trying to push more magic into it, to get it moving again. But it was stuck fast as if paused on purpose.

She looked back at the draugr, who was still standing there by its statue. But this time the creature's eyes weren't on the two sisters by the river. It was looking at something behind them.

Or make that . . . someone.

"Look!" Anna cried, pointing. "Who's that?"

Elsa squinted at the figure, standing motionless, encased in ice. It appeared to be a young boy—around fourteen or fifteen years of age. He had shaggy hair and big eyes and was carrying a shepherd's crook. In fact, she realized, as her eyes dropped lower, there was a lamb at his feet.

"Whoa," she whispered.

"It's the witness!" Anna cried. "From Kristoff's story! I totally forgot until now, but he said there was a witness! That's how they were able to prove Inger's crime!" She turned back to Elsa. "Make the memory move again. Let's see if he says anything."

Elsa bit her lower lip. "Um, I didn't stop it to begin with." She glanced over at the draugr. "Can you show us more?"

The creature seemed to nod. The vision leapt back to life. Inger's screams once again reached their ears.

"Help me!" she was crying to the boy. "Help me save my sister! Please!"

"Stay where you are," the boy shouted. "You'll be swept away, too!" He ran to the shore, leaning over the water, wrapping his hand around a tree to anchor himself. He tried to grab the other end of the branch Sissel was clinging to, but it was just out of his reach. Inger stood watching, helpless and scared.

"Come on, Sissel," she whispered. "Just hold on."

Sissel looked up at her younger sister. Her brown eyes

no longer reflected her fear, but rather a strange sense of resolve. Elsa cringed, realizing the truth. At that very moment, Sissel had known she was going to die. And she had accepted her fate.

"I love you, Inger," Sissel said. "And I believe in you. I know you will do me proud."

"NO!" Inger begged, her face twisted with horror. "Don't leave me, Sissel!" Her voice cracked on the words. "I can't do this without you!"

But her sister only shook her head. "Yes, you can," she said solemnly. Her voice no longer sounded afraid, but determined. "You can do anything." She paused, then added, "You're my sister. And you're stronger than you know."

And with that, the branch broke free. Sissel's body was tossed like a rag doll over the falls. Inger screamed in agony, collapsing to the ground, sobs wracking her body.

"Sissel," she cried out. "Oh, my sweet Sissel."

A moment later the shepherd boy was by her side. He tried to help her get up, but Inger's legs refused to work. She kept staring at the raging river, her whole body trembling with grief. The boy reached down, gently swiping a lock of hair from her face, meeting her eyes with his own.

"What's your name?" he said gently.

"Inger," she whispered, clinging to his hand.

He nodded. "Inger, I'm Stig. I'm going to help you," he said.

And just like that, the vision faded. The raging river went quiet again.

Elsa turned slowly back to the draugr. It was still standing by the shore, staring at the water. It took Elsa a moment to realize the creature's cheeks were wet.

It was crying. *She* was crying.

"Your sister didn't murder you," Anna whispered. "That's what you've been trying to tell us, isn't it? Everyone's been spreading a false story! You want them to know the truth. It was an accident. Your sister was innocent all along. She loved you. And you loved her."

Sissel nodded, staring forlornly at the river. Elsa felt her heart go out to the creature, and suddenly she half wanted to run over and give her a warm hug. They'd been afraid of the draugr for so long. But now she felt only pity as she gazed on the grotesque creature. For Inger, too, who had been accused of a crime she hadn't committed.

To lose your sister like that had to feel like you'd lost one of your own limbs. Elsa could only hope this was a pain she'd never have to go through herself.

Because to lose Anna . . . her Anna . . .

She shook her head. No. She wouldn't even think of it. She couldn't.

Elsa looked up at the draugr again. "You were trying to share this memory with me earlier, weren't you?" she asked, realization washing over her. "When we met you in the forest. You grabbed my hand. I thought you were trying to erase my memories. But you were trying to share your own." She gave an apologetic shrug. "I'm sorry I didn't understand."

The draugr shuffled from foot to foot, moaning softly. Elsa decided to take that as forgiveness. She turned back to Anna.

"At least now we know the whole story," she said. "What really happened."

"Do we, though?" Anna asked, scratching her head as she looked from the draugr to the memorial upstream. "Why did Inger get blamed for it all? I mean, there was a witness! Why didn't she and that boy, Stig, just go back and tell people what really happened? Her name would have been cleared!"

Sissel moaned, shaking her head. She clearly didn't know why—she had died before that part of the story happened. Leaving yet another mystery to solve, Elsa realized. Just one more mystery in this whole thing.

"Don't worry," she told Sissel. "We're going to figure this out. Somehow. And then we'll tell everyone the truth. What really happened. Clear your sister's name once and for all."

The draugr's eyes seemed to brighten. *"Sissssster,"* she moaned, seeming to agree. *"Sissssster mine . . ."* And with that, she began to shuffle off into the woods.

Elsa and Anna watched her go, amazed.

"Guess we know what the draugr wants now," Anna said.

"*And* we know where to go next," Elsa agreed. "To find the one person who might still be alive. The one person who was really there."

"Stig," Anna said. "And I know just how to track him down."

CHAPTER SIXTEEN

Anna

ANNA AND ELSA RODE LIKE the Wind Spirit—fast, without stopping—not talking till they reached a stormy Arendelle. Rain and snow were mixing as sleet pooled on the cobblestone streets and thunder continued to boom overhead. But there was no time to focus on the weather. The pair didn't stop till they were safely inside the darkened castle.

"You're back!" Olaf cried, hurrying down the staircase to meet them. "Good morning! Or should I say, 'good night'? It's getting really dark here," he added, worry written all over his face. "But the good news is there have been no draugr sightings since you left. And we have the pirate situation completely under control!"

Anna slapped her head and groaned. "That's right! The pirates!" She hesitated, wanting to go back down the stairs, out of the castle, and straight to the port. "Are they actually here? In Arendelle? What's going on? Are they stopping our ships from coming in and out of port?" A flash of lightning lit up the room.

"The storms are stopping our ships, actually." Olaf touched her hand. "But thankfully they're keeping the pirates at bay, too. At least for now."

Well, thank you, Sissel, Anna said to herself. At least that gave them some time to help Sissel before dealing with the pirates. Got it.

Being a queen was exhausting sometimes.

"Your Majesty!" Mattias appeared at the foot of the stairs and stood at attention. "I have stationed our guards around the port. Any pirate dares approach and they'll live to regret it." He cleared his throat. "And we will send word to their captain that we would like a meeting as soon as the storms let up, as you requested."

"Well, that's good," Anna reasoned. Though she hadn't actually requested anything, obviously. Mattias's memory was clearly as bad as the others. But at least he was now acting like a general again. "Please send word if anything changes."

Mattias looked at her strangely, then glanced at Olaf.

"You can go do your general stuff," Olaf said. Mattias nodded and disappeared around a corner. Anna shot a look at Elsa. They *really* needed to clear this Sissel thing up—and fast!

Olaf's eyes lit up. "So where are you going? Can I come? And . . . not be left alone for Sinister Sissel to find?"

Elsa picked Olaf up. "First, let's stop calling Sissel sinister. We're pretty sure she's not trying to harm us. She actually needs our help."

"Oh, and her sister didn't murder her, either, turns out," Anna added. When Olaf's eyes widened, she shrugged. "We'll fill you in, but it's a long story. First, we need to find Stig."

"Stig?" Olaf asked. "I don't remember any Stig." He stopped short. "Oh no! Is my memory going, too?"

"No, no! You don't know him. None of us do. But he was there the day Sissel drowned, and he might have some answers as to why Inger was blamed."

"We're hoping we can find him listed in the census and figure out where he lives." Anna bit her lower lip. "If he's still alive . . ."

"Then what are we waiting for?" Olaf asked, jumping down and toddling away. "Let's go find this *sentence*! I mean, census! That's a book, right?"

The trio headed to Anna's private study, which had belonged to Elsa and their father before them. Probably Runeard as well, once upon a time, though Anna didn't like to think about their grandfather seated in the same old, cracked leather chair that she used now. She hadn't mentioned this to Elsa yet, but she was getting a sneaking suspicion something about this whole mess was at least partially their grandfather's doing. After all, he was why Sissel and Inger had come to Arendelle to begin with.

"Luckily, they only do a census every ten or more years," Elsa said as she opened one of the books and went to the most recent record. Her finger slid along each listing, which cataloged people by the farms or properties they lived on, their jobs, and their ages and marital status, along with birth and death dates and lists of the other members of the household. "Let's see how many people named Stig used to be shepherds and are around sixty-five years old." She shook her head. "This could take a bit, since everything's listed by last name."

"Which is why we also need to look in these court records," said Anna as she pulled out a thick bound book. "Since we know when the sisters visited Arendelle, I can narrow it down." She flipped through the pages, looking for the correct year, and soon found the Vesterland sisters' names. "This is it! Inger's hearing!" Elsa and Olaf came over to look.

"'Witness, Stig Petter,'" Elsa read. "Perfect. I'll just—"

"Whoa," Anna interrupted, her eyes skimming the page. "No way."

"What is it?" Elsa asked.

Anna sat back. "He lied. Stig lied!"

"What?" Elsa stared down at the record in disbelief.

"According to this, Stig reported seeing Inger push Sissel into the water and watch her drown," Anna summarized. "Inger denied the claim, but as Stig was the lone witness, the court sided with him." She closed the book, stunned. "Why would he lie? He was right there! He saw the whole thing!"

"Stig Petter, what are you hiding?" Elsa murmured, going back to the census and scanning the listings with her fingers. "Here he is! He's still alive," she said, relieved. "But it looks like he doesn't live in Arendelle anymore."

"Where does he live?" Anna asked, her heart sinking a little. Hopefully it wasn't too far.

"In the mountains. Just outside the village of Harmon."

Okay, that wasn't far. And also? Maybe since he was outside of Arendelle, Stig wouldn't have lost his memory like everyone here had.

It was a long shot. But it was the only one they had.

Please, Stig, Anna thought when they finally arrived at his cottage after battling more wind and rain. *Help us get to the bottom of this mystery.* Unfortunately, she wasn't hopeful he was going to be a very cooperative witness. After all, he'd lied years ago. What if he continued to stick to his story now? He was their last hope; the one person who had been there—seen everything. Somehow they had to convince him to help them. Or Sissel might never find peace.

And Arendelle would be cast into stormy darkness forever.

Anna slid off her horse while Elsa quickly dismounted the Water Nokk and the two of them hurried to the door, rapping hard to be heard over the thunder. A moment later, the door flew open. An older man with wire-rim spectacles and a bald head, tufts of white hair over his ears, stared at them angrily.

"What are you doing out in weather like this?" he demanded in a gruff voice.

"Mr. Petter?" Anna asked eagerly as water dripped off her nose. "Stig Petter?"

"Yes," he said, sounding cranky. "That's my name, and yours is Queen Anna, and hers is Queen Elsa. What I don't know is why you're at my door."

"Something is happening in Arendelle that we could use your help with," Elsa informed him, giving him a hopeful smile. "Can we come in?"

"Sorry," Stig said, looking suddenly nervous. "I can't help you." He made a move to shut his door.

"Please?" Anna begged as a crack of thunder made the group jump. "Just let us in for a moment. We're soaked to the bone."

Stig sighed. "Fine. Get in here, then. But don't expect anything further from me. I left Arendelle fifty years ago. And I have no interest in the kingdom's affairs."

That didn't sound promising. But at least he was letting them in. Maybe Anna could work on him a little more once he heard how dire the situation was. And at least it would get them out of the rain. The two girls quickly moved into the cottage, and Stig shut the door behind them. It was a humble space with a fire roaring and a pot over the hearth that was bubbling with some sort of soup. Unlike at the Figels' house, this soup smelled delicious.

"Thank you," Elsa said, wringing out the bottom of her dress. "We don't mean to impose."

"We just had a few questions for you about something that happened when you were a young man," Anna told him as she wiped her wet hands on her skirt. She was so tired of being wet all the time.

Stig's expression darkened. "If you're asking how I got the funds for this cottage when I stopped herding sheep, that's none of your business! It's like I told everyone else—I don't owe you any explanations! I inherited this cottage fair and . . . square." His voice trailed off.

"This isn't about the cottage," Elsa told him.

"Oh," Stig said, still sounding uncomfortable. "Then what is it you want to know?"

Anna decided to go for broke. "We want to know about Princess Inger. We know you were there the day she and her sister argued at the riverbank and Sissel was swept away." Anna tried to sound calm. Rational. Like she was asking a simple question about the weather. But inside, she was angry—Stig had lied, and his lie had destroyed a young girl's life! Why had he done it? And would he admit to it now—fifty years later?

Stig stiffened. "I don't know what you're talking about," he muttered. But his cheeks were quite red. Another lie, Anna presumed.

"Come on. We saw the whole thing in a memory I created," Elsa broke in. "We know that Sissel fell in while trying to save Inger, and that you were there and tried to help save her. When you couldn't, you went back and comforted Inger."

"You told her you were going to help her!" Anna

added indignantly. "And then you went and accused her of murder! Publicly! Because of you, she was sentenced to death! For something you know she didn't do!"

Stig's face hardened. "You have to leave. Now," he said, guiding Anna by the arm to the door. "I'm sorry, Your Majesties, but I have made my peace with this matter." His voice caught. "I never want to hear the Vesterland sisters' names again."

Anna was so close she could see the deep wrinkles in his forehead and the windburn on his chapped cheeks. His blue eyes were almost gray with age and held so much fear. Something had happened that day that haunted him. But what? Why would he lie about Inger? Why did he live up here alone, hidden away from the world, and bristle at talk of how he paid for his cottage, unless . . .

Suddenly she remembered her hunch back at the castle. She turned to face Stig and tried to take a different approach. "Someone asked you to lie about Inger, didn't they?" she said gently, not really making it a question.

Stig looked away, not answering her, which told her she was probably right.

"But who would do that?" Elsa asked, turning to her sister in confusion.

"Isn't it obvious? Our grandfather," Anna pronounced. "With Sissel dead and Inger being held for her murder, the Vesterland sisters couldn't oppose the dam," she explained. "You heard them in that memory—they wanted to go back and stand up to Grandfather. Inger convinced Sissel not to help fund the dam, and they could have rallied other nearby kingdoms, too, which would have meant Arendelle wouldn't have the funding to build." She drew in a breath. "Grandfather couldn't allow that to happen."

"That's horrible," Elsa whispered. "And yet, it makes sense. Even with Sissel gone, Inger never would have stopped fighting Grandfather on the dam." She glanced at Stig. "If he had a witness willing to say Inger pushed Sissel in the river, neither sister would ever be a problem for him again."

Stig placed his face in his hands. A single tear slipped down his cheek. When he finally looked up, the hurt in his face was visible. "You're right. I lied then. And now, fifty years later, those lies are still haunting me." He grabbed a handkerchief and blew into it loudly. "Trust me, I'll never forgive myself for what I did to that poor, sweet girl, but it's too late to do anything about it now."

"Actually, that might not be true," said Anna as she took his hand and led him to a chair. "Let's talk. So, King Runeard told you to lie?"

"Yes," Stig said, his voice shaking. It took him a moment before he spoke again. Anna waited patiently. "I wasn't planning to lie at first. I told the king exactly what happened. Inger was beside herself when Sissel was swept away. She and I ran back to the village for help, but of course there was nothing we could do." Anna squeezed his hand. "It was only after the king met with Inger that something changed . . ." His voice trailed off.

"Go on, "Elsa urged gently. "It's okay."

"Runeard called for me again and told me that I was wrong about Inger—that I was to tell the world I saw her murder her sister." He covered his face with his hands again. "He told me if I said otherwise, he'd inform people I helped Inger do it and have me sent to prison for life." His voice cracked. "I said I'd speak out and tell everyone how he threatened me, but the king just laughed." He glanced into the distance, his eyes glazing over. "I remember he said, 'Who is going to believe you? You're nothing but a poor shepherd.' "

"That's despicable!" Anna said angrily. "Your king shouldn't have threatened you."

"I know, but what could I do?" Stig said hoarsely. "I could either lie or face jail—or worse. So I did what I was told, and the king rewarded me for my lie. I no longer had to be a sheepherder. I had enough money to buy this place and hide away here."

He motioned to the cottage around him, and Elsa and Anna were quiet, listening to the rain pound the cottage's roof.

"I was too ashamed to be part of village life after that," Stig said. "I was afraid someone would ask me about the Vesterland sisters and I'd slip, so I've stayed away all these years while the guilt has eaten at me from the inside out. Those two sisters have haunted my dreams for years." He closed his eyes. "Sometimes, I feel like I can still hear Inger calling out to Sissel on that riverbank so long ago." The old man broke down in tears.

Anna felt anger rise inside of her all over again. But this time it was not directed at Stig. He had been a victim as much as the two sisters, she realized. And though he hadn't done the right thing at the time, it was pretty understandable why. She put her arm around the shepherd, trying to comfort him as best she could as she looked up to her sister, who appeared deep in thought. "It all makes sense," she said softly. "Why everyone has the story wrong. Our grandfather made sure of it."

"And now Sissel wants the story set straight," Elsa agreed. "And she wants us to do it."

Stig looked up, surprised. "Wait. Are you saying Sissel is still alive? But I saw her drown! There's no way she could have survived that waterfall!"

Anna hesitated. She wasn't sure how much more Stig could take, but . . .

"Yes and no. Sissel has become a draugr, and she's haunting Arendelle and stealing memories to try to make people stop thinking Inger murdered her. She's what's causing this weather and the darkness."

Stig's jaw fell. "A draugr?" he whispered.

"Yes, but if you come forward, Sissel might finally rest," Elsa told him. "Like Grand Pabbie said, '*To end this all, you must tell her tale*.' You need to tell people the truth about Inger."

Stig thought for a moment. "I don't know if they'll listen to an old shepherd, but I guess I could try. I owe

Inger that much. Maybe she'll even forgive me. Though I wouldn't blame her if she didn't." He stared down at the cottage floor, looking sad.

Anna shot Elsa a look. "I hate to tell you this," she said gently, "but Inger can't forgive you. She's dead, too."

Stig's head jerked. His eyes locked on the sisters. "Yes, that's what people think," he said. "But in truth, she's very much alive. And from what I understand, she's not far away, either."

CHAPTER SEVENTEEN

Elsa

"ALIVE?" ELSA REPEATED, staring at Stig in shock. "But we were told the prison ship carrying her was lost at sea before it could reach its destination!" Had they gotten this part of the story wrong, too? But, no, this was written down in official Arendelle records.

Then again, so was Inger's supposed crime.

Stig shrugged sheepishly. "The prison ship may have gone down, but Inger was never on it," he told them, sitting up straighter in his chair. "Your grandmother helped her escape before it ever set sail."

"Our *grandmother*?" Anna repeated, eyes widening. "You mean Queen Rita?"

The girls didn't know much about their grandmother on their father's side. From Ahtohallan, Elsa had learned that Rita had escaped Arendelle when their father was just a child because she was unhappy with her marriage and her life. No one, however, knew what happened to her.

"Queen Rita was the only one who believed Inger," Stig explained. "She knew what a bad man your grandfather was, and she had spent time with both sisters. She probably realized Inger would never do what she was accused of. In fact, I saw her try to speak up for Inger in court, but Runeard quickly shut her down, sending her to her chambers. She had to have known nothing she said would change what was happening, and in fact, it might even make it worse. But she could help in another way."

"So she helped Inger escape?"

"Yes. I watched her do it. I was feeling guilty about what I'd done, and I was roaming the streets of Arendelle after not being able to sleep. I saw Queen Rita standing on the docks by the prison ship, accompanied by a couple fierce-looking men and Inger herself. Inger was cloaked in black, so I didn't recognize her at first. But then I saw her eyes. Inger had such blue eyes—I'd know them anywhere. From what I overheard them saying, the queen had paid the men to steal Inger off the ship and give her safe passage on another. Queen Rita told Inger she should leave and never come back. If she did, she'd surely be put to death."

"Wow." Elsa gave a low whistle. "Go Grandma!"

Stig nodded. "I overheard Inger make a vow that night, before boarding the ship. She told your grandmother that she would sail the ocean—until her dying day, if necessary—to find her sister's body and put it in a rightful grave. Only then could they both rest in peace."

"And you think she could still be out there?" Anna asked. "I mean, this was fifty years ago. Even if she did survive all this time, she'd be very old."

"She is. But she's still carrying out the vow she made that night. Right off the shores of Arendelle, actually, from what I've read."

Elsa looked at him in confusion. "What are you talking about?"

Stig reached over to a small cabinet and pulled open a drawer. Elsa and Anna watched as he lifted up a copy of the *Village Crown* and spread it out over the table. Then he pointed to the headline:

COULD "OLD BLUE EYES"

BE HEADED FOR ARENDELLE?

Elsa gasped, her gaze rising to her sister. From the look on Anna's face, she realized she must have been thinking the same thing.

Stig tapped his fingers on the image of the blue-eyed pirate queen. "She's older, of course. And her hair is different. But those eyes—those eyes have haunted my dreams for fifty years." He looked up at the girls. "That's Inger. I'd swear my life on it."

"I can't believe it! She was right under our noses the whole time!" Anna paced the deck of the ship as the sailors readied its sails and riggings. After learning Inger's new identity from Stig, she and Elsa had rushed back to Arendelle and urged the crew to prepare to set sail for the pirate ships under the guise that they wanted to negotiate with them. Stig had promised to meet them in the village to tell the people the truth about what had happened to Sissel, which was great. But what a bonus it would be to actually have Inger hear him do it. So she'd know she'd been vindicated in the end.

Speaking of sisters, Elsa watched as Anna stared down at the copy of the *Village Crown* with her article on the front page, just beneath the one on the blue-eyed Pirate Queen. "Here I thought Sissel was reading about *me* when she picked up my copy of the paper! But she was looking at her sister! I mean, she literally said, 'Sister'!" Anna groaned. "I feel like such an idiot."

"You couldn't have known," Elsa comforted, though she was feeling a little annoyed herself for not making the connection. Now that they had compared the article with the past pictures of Inger, the resemblance was unmistakable—give or take fifty years. "We thought she was dead."

"Yeah," Anna agreed. "That's true." She sighed. "I hope at least she'll agree to talk to us. And not make us walk the plank or something." She shuddered.

"Are you sure you want to do this?" Erik, the ship's

captain, asked, stepping up to them. His face was grave. He hadn't liked the idea of sailing out to meet the pirates, especially in this weather. But somehow Olaf had convinced him to gather the crew and set sail. (The snowman himself decided to stay on solid ground. Someone had to keep an eye on Arendelle, after all!)

The weather had actually gotten worse by the time they headed out to sea, and the sailors struggled to steer into the thickening storm. Gale helped all it could, blowing fresh wind into the sails in the right direction, while the Water Nokk ran in front of them, clearing a path in the wild seas. The rain was coming down in torrents, and they had to grab on to the sides of the ship to keep upright.

Fortunately, the pirate fleet was not too far off the coast, and soon they could see the ships' black flags whipping in the wind from their masts. Elsa felt a shiver slip down her spine that had nothing to do with the fact that she was freezing and soaking wet.

"Slow your approach," Anna called to the sailors, who also looked apprehensive. "Raise the white flag. Let them know we're on a peace mission."

The sailors ran to obey, but before they could, they heard a loud boom. Fire flashed from the sky, and a moment later there was a huge splash that covered the entire deck.

"They're shooting their cannons at us!" Anna cried, horrified. She called out a new order to the sailors. "Don't go any closer."

"Clearly they're not interested in peace treaties," Elsa muttered.

"How are we going to talk to Inger if we can't even get close to her?" Anna wondered.

"You are going to stay here. I'm going out there myself." Elsa headed to the side of the ship.

Anna grabbed her arm. "What? You can't. They'll kill you!"

"It'll be a lot harder to hit me with cannons on the Water Nokk than on a big ship. I'll get there, don't worry. And I'll let them know we mean no harm. Then we can get you on board."

Anna clenched her hands together tightly. Elsa could tell she wanted to argue, but at the same time, she was trying to trust her big sister. To be fair, Elsa wasn't entirely sure she should trust herself at this point, but they had little choice. She had to get close enough to the pirates to talk to them. And this was the only way to do it.

She whistled for the Water Spirit. A moment later it leapt from the depths of the sea, splashing the side of the ship. Elsa climbed onto its back, taking the reins with an expert hand. She pressed her thighs against the cold flanks of the water horse and lowered her head.

"Okay," she whispered. "Get me to those ships!"

The Water Nokk whinnied in agreement, then took off galloping, with Elsa using her powers to turn the water into ice as they went to keep them above the violent sea.

BOOM!

Another cannon exploded with fire as the pirates took aim again—this time at her. The ice in front of them erupted as the iron ball hit its mark, shattering the frozen path into a thousand pieces. The Water Nokk reared back on two legs, snorting furiously. Elsa shot another pathway of ice, this time to the right side, and urged the Water Spirit on further.

"Come on!" she cried. "We have to keep going!"

The Water Nokk charged forward again, and once more the cannon boomed, its salvo smashing closer this time, icy water shooting up and dousing Elsa. She gripped the spirit's neck as hard as she could and shot a new ice pathway to their left. But it was harder to do it this time, and the ice came out more as a trickle than a spray. She worried her powers were starting to deplete again thanks to her earlier encounter with the draugr. And if they sputtered out entirely when she was out in the middle of the ocean, there'd be nowhere to go but into the sea.

Her mind raced with indecision. Should she keep going forward or turn back, hoping to reach their own ship again before she became completely powerless? If she turned around, she'd have failed. They'd never stop the draugr. Arendelle would be lost in darkness forever.

No. That couldn't happen. The people were counting on her. Anna was counting on her.

A sudden thought came to her. She whistled to Gale. The Wind Spirit swept up around her, clearly concerned.

"Go to the pirate ships," she instructed. "Fill their sails and send them to me."

Gale swept up a spray of seawater in agreement, then took off across the water. A moment later, she watched the ships being pushed forward, toward her, at high speed. She could see women and men on the decks scrambling at the sudden gust out of nowhere and heard them calling out in alarm. They were distracted. They wouldn't fire again until they got their ships sorted. Which gave her a chance.

Elsa patted the horse's neck. "Okay," she said. "One more push. You can do this!"

The spirit leapt forward as Elsa shot ice across the sea, making a bridge between them and the closest ship. The Water Nokk was running so fast Elsa's vision blurred with tears and her cheeks stung from the salt spray. But she held on tight, as tight as she could, thinking of Inger and Sissel . . . and Anna. And all the people of Arendelle.

She was the Snow Queen. She could do this.

As she grew nearer, she could hear the pirates shouting from the ship's deck.

"What is it?"

"Is it a siren?"

"A mermaid?"

"She's riding a horse!"

"That doesn't look like any horse I've ever seen."

Elsa opened her eyes and realized they had stopped just below the largest of the pirate ships. Several crew members were staring down at her, eyes bulging in shock.

She smiled weakly at them. "Hello," she said. "My name is Elsa. I mean you no harm." She could feel the ice beginning to crack under the Water Nokk's feet. "Please. If you don't mind, may I board your ship?"

They glanced at one another as if unsure. Then there was rustling. Someone was pushing through the crowd, which parted in reverence. Whoever it was must be a leader. Could it be Inger?

Elsa watched, wide-eyed, as a young woman around her age stepped to the bow of the ship and looked down at her. She was dressed in a leather tunic tied with a red sash, and wore a pirate hat over shocking red hair.

And she had very, very blue eyes.

Elsa gasped. "Inger?" she whispered. It didn't make any sense; Inger should have been seventy years old. But there could be no mistaking the resemblance. "Is that you?"

"Actually," the woman said, "my name is Sissel."

CHAPTER EIGHTEEN

Anna

"WHAT IS HAPPENING?" Anna mumbled to herself, watching the choppy water as the tiny figure of Elsa jumped off the Water Nokk and onto the deck of a pirate ship that could become hostile at any moment. *Toward her sister.*

Anna's heart was in her throat. She knew Elsa could handle herself. She knew the Water Spirit could move more swiftly than the wind and dodge cannon fire, but still . . . that hardly placated her deep worries. The storm was raging, the boat was rocking violently, and she could hear the pirates' shouts echoing across the wind—even at this distance.

"She shouldn't be out there alone!" Anna exclaimed to Captain Erik as she watched Elsa approach a large group of pirates.

"Probably not," Captain Erik agreed as a giant swell rocked their boat and practically sent it sideways. They both grabbed tightly to whatever they could to make sure they stayed on their feet. "Those pirates don't look friendly. Then again, I don't think they worry about being hospitable."

"Of course not! That's why she shouldn't be so reckless and try to do these things alone! I should have insisted I go with her!" Anna grumbled.

Over on the pirate ship, Elsa was motioning wildly with her hands, and Anna could only assume her sister was trying to explain herself. "I'm a fast talker," she added, in case Erik didn't remember under the circumstances. "I hold the record in talking, thank you very much. If anyone could get through to those pirates, it would be—*OH*. Wait. What's going on? It's so hard to see!" Anna held her hand up to shield her eyes as the rain came down harder. A flash of lightning lit up the sky, allowing her a brief glimpse of the action on the pirate ship deck.

Erik held up a bronze spyglass. "It looks like they're letting her through to talk to . . . is that their pirate captain?"

Anna reached for the spyglass and saw Elsa talking to a female pirate wearing a large hat. A woman with red hair who looked weirdly familiar. She gasped. Had Elsa found Inger? No, she looked too young, didn't she? Anna strained to see more, but the rain was making it impossible. Anna sighed, frustrated. Elsa was okay, which was good, but what were they talking about? Was Inger on the ship? "If only I could get over there!" she said in exasperation.

"Looks like they're coming to us instead!" Erik shouted as the pirate ships began to make their way through the rocky fjord straight for their smaller boat. They were coming in so fast between the waves and the storm, Anna was sure they were going to crash, but the pirate ships navigated the waters as expertly as the Arendellian navy; Anna could only assume it was through Gale's doing. They pulled up and dropped anchor, and the next thing Anna knew, they were lowering a plank and beckoning her to come aboard.

"Is it her?" Anna blurted out as Elsa held out a hand

and helped her onto the pirate ship. "Did you find her? Did she say anything?" The questions came tumbling out of her, much like the waves that were making her seasick.

"Anna, meet Inger's granddaughter." Elsa motioned to the young woman in the oversized hat. "This is Sissel."

Anna inhaled sharply, her stomach doing a giant flip. "Sissel?"

"Call me Red. Everyone does." The girl tipped her hat and smiled, revealing a gold tooth. Anna could see the resemblance. While the girl might have been named for the great-aunt she had never met, she was the spitting image of her grandmother. She had the same piercing blue eyes everyone always mentioned Inger had.

Red nodded and stood up straighter. "Yes, and my grandmother Inger has put me in charge of this vessel. Elsa explained you need to see her right away." Her eyes flitted around the deck warily. "But I'm not sure she's up to visitors. She's getting up there in years and leaves the trade negotiations up to me."

"This isn't about a trade agreement, though as queen I will have to discuss that matter eventually," Anna said, feeling brave. "But first we wanted to talk to her about a personal matter." Anna looked at Elsa. "We have news about her sister."

"You mean my great-aunt Sissel? My namesake?" Red's eyes widened. "Have you found her body? We've been looking for her up and down the seaboard for years!" Her expression softened. "That's why we're back in Arendelle actually. Well, we come every year for the anniversary of Sissel's death. But we usually leave after a little memorial service—so as not to freak everyone on shore out. This time, however, my grandmother claims she's been seeing her sister in her dreams this past week, calling to her. And so she's refused to let us leave, insisting she's here somewhere. I thought she was just getting senile in her old age. But if you have news . . ."

A large boom of thunder made everyone jump. Water splashed over the deck as the ship careened left then right before leveling off again. The storm was worsening by the second. Anna had only been through a storm as bad as this once before—the ice storm created by Elsa that fateful coronation day.

How funny, she thought suddenly. What if the way

to stop this whole thing was in the very same manner that she and Elsa had stopped their storm the first time around?

Through the love of two sisters.

"We know where Sissel is, and we promise to explain everything once you bring us to your grandmother," Anna declared.

Red thought for a moment. "All right. This way," she said, leading them to a large hatch embedded in the deck of the ship. The door was hand-carved and featured a scene of a ship fighting a kraken. Red leaned down and yanked on the handle, and the door groaned as it opened, revealing a rickety staircase leading belowdecks. The air smelled like gunpowder. Red began to descend, then looked up at them. "Come on. She's down here."

Anna and Elsa followed her down the steps into the darkness. The ship tossed and turned in the storm, making it difficult to walk down the dark hall, which was lit by flickering lanterns. Red seemed to have no issue, however, walking as steadily as if she were on dry land. But then, she had probably been born with sea legs.

She led them through a few small sleeping quarters furnished with swinging hammocks before they came upon a small bedroom at the back of the ship, clearly built for a captain. Inside, they found an old woman, lying in bed, fast asleep. She had long white braids and a leathered, wind-chapped face, but that wasn't what told Anna for certain they had found Inger. It was the black-and-white sketches pinned up all over the room. There were dozens of them, all depicting the same girl; her hair fashioned in a bob, her dresses elegant, her face smiling and young, forever the age she had been when they saw her in Elsa's ice memory.

"Anna, look, it's Sissel," Elsa whispered. Her hands touched a piece of parchment on the wall with a sketch of Sissel sitting on a rock looking out at the water. She clasped Anna's hand. "We've found both Vesterland sisters."

Yes, Anna thought. *Now if only we can help them before it's too late.*

"Gam?" Red whispered. "Are you awake?"

"I'm always awake," the old woman croaked. Her eyes fluttered open, revealing her famous startling blues. "You're still my protégée, my pet, and I need to keep an eye on you even when my eyes are closed."

Red chuckled and looked at Anna and Elsa. "As you

can see, while she struggles to get out of bed, her mind is fully intact."

"Princess Inger? Of Vesterland?" Anna asked even though she knew for sure it was her. She just needed the woman to say the words aloud.

Inger's lips pursed. "Who is asking and why? Not that I think you'd have much hope of taking me in for questioning at this age. I'd turn to dust before you could even hold a trial."

"Gammy, stop talking like that." Red bristled. "You'll be around forever."

Inger huffed. "Sure feels like it." She looked at Anna and Elsa. "But I won't spend my final years in a cell. Take these two away."

"No! Wait!" Elsa cried. "We're not here to arrest you."

"We're here to help you," Anna added.

"Help?" Inger raised her right eyebrow. "Now that's a word I haven't heard in a long time. Not since Queen Rita of this very kingdom snuck me aboard this very ship."

"That's our grandmother," Anna said proudly.

"This is Queen Anna and Queen Elsa of Arendelle," Red explained.

Inger sat up at the news. "Is it now? Well, then, you

should know it was your grandmother who saved my life. Your grandfather would have had me sent to the gallows."

Elsa shuffled uncomfortably. "Yeah, we tend to do a lot of apologizing on his behalf."

"The world thinks I left on a prison ship, which I later heard went down at sea," Inger said. "The truth is your grandmother bought me safe passage on a different vessel that was soon boarded by pirates."

"Tell them what happened," Red insisted.

Inger looked at Elsa and Anna. "The crew quickly locked me up, but not for long." She tapped her head. "I've always had a mind for science, so I quickly wooed them with knowledge of charting courses, how wind affects speed, and how to measure water depths." She shrugged. "They couldn't resist me."

Red chuckled. "She's always been cheeky. It's what Grandpappy loved about her."

"Aye, he did," Inger said. "When I met Dag, he was quite ornery for a captain. I won him over and became his apprentice, then eventually his wife. I helped him loosen up and not take life too seriously, like my sister always . . ."

Inger trailed off. *Clearly Sissel is still a sore subject,* Anna thought.

"They had my mother, who later had me, and named me after the great-aunt I never knew," Red told them. "And now I run this ship with Gam."

"You're an apprentice," Inger told her sharply. "But a good one at that."

"And you've been at sea ever since." Anna's eyes flickered to the drawings on the wall.

Inger's face fell. "I've been up and down this seaboard searching for her. For years, I thought maybe she'd survived the river. I imagined she hit her head, forgot who she was, and was wandering around on some unknown shore just waiting to be found by me." Her voice softened. "But now my hope is just to retrieve her body and give her a proper burial, if someone hasn't already." She closed her eyes. "Once I do that, then I can rest. We both can. Together."

Elsa looked at Anna. Their story was so sad. Anna didn't want to imagine what her life would be like if Elsa wasn't in it. "I'm so sorry for all you've been through, Inger," Anna said. "But we're here because we can help clear your name. We know you didn't push her in the river."

Inger closed her eyes as if in pain. "You're the only one who believes that. There was even a witness at the river that day, but he lied to King Runeard about what he saw."

"Stig," Anna said, her voice hardening. "We've found him, too. It turns out our grandfather forced him to lie. He feels terrible for what he did, and he's finally ready to come forward and tell everyone what he saw."

"How did you track him down and get him to confess?" Red asked.

"I'm the Snow Queen," Elsa explained. "I was born with the power of snow and ice. And, because water has memory, I was able to see what really happened that day by the river."

Inger looked at her. "The Snow Queen . . . I've heard many stories about your gift. I never thought I'd see the day when I'd receive one." Inger leaned forward and reached for Elsa's hand. "But I don't care about me. I just want to find my sister." She trailed off, but then sudden hope sparked in her blue eyes. "Do you know where her body is?"

Anna stiffened. How would she explain what Sissel had become? She turned to Elsa. "That's just it. Sissel was never buried, so she . . ." Anna hesitated and looked at Elsa.

"She what?" Inger pressed.

"She came back as a draugr," Elsa finished.

Red gasped and Inger leaned into her granddaughter's body.

"No," she whispered, crying softly. "My poor sister. Where is she? I need to see her."

"Gammy, no," Red insisted. "Not like this. She's a monster."

"Monster or not, she's my sister," Inger said defiantly. "If anyone can help her find peace, it's me." She looked at Anna and Elsa. "Can you take me to her? Do you know how to find her again?"

The ship lurched sideways, sending the group tumbling. Anna could hear yelling from above on deck.

"We think so," Anna said. "But we have to hurry. I don't have time to explain, but if we're going to save your sister and help her find peace, we need to go now."

CHAPTER NINETEEN

Elsa

"COME ON, GALE! HURRY!"

Elsa glanced nervously up at the dark, stormy sky, the wind whipping through her hair, making her wish she'd tied it back up in a braid. At least it was no longer raining or snowing. Still, they'd been trying to fight their way through the choppy waters back to Arendelle for what felt like hours now, but the winds were not cooperating. Instead, they were tossing the ship like a toy boat and making her stomach go topsy-turvy.

Gale was doing its best to move the boat along, but even the Wind Spirit was having trouble making headway against the storm. And the Water Nokk was having no luck navigating the rough seas, which seemed to be unimpressed by the spirit's attempts.

"You should go belowdecks with the others," Captain Erik commanded, having to shout over the wind. "It's not safe out here." The crew was running from side to side, yelling at one another; even their sea legs were looking unsure.

Elsa nodded stiffly. "I'm all right," she assured him. "I need to make sure Gale and the Water Nokk don't need any help." Not that ice powers were all that useful in a situation like this.

For a moment she imagined her parents, in a similar storm, on a similar ship, just before it went down. And they hadn't had magical spirits to help them stay afloat. At what moment had they realized they weren't going to make it? Elsa still felt a little guilty about the fact that they'd gone out to the Dark Sea to try to help her. But she knew, in her heart, if she'd been in their shoes, she would have made the same choice to help them.

They had done their best to save her. And now she and her sister would save Arendelle.

If they could reach it in time.

"Land ho!"

Suddenly a voice cut through the wind from the ship's crow's nest above. Elsa stumbled to the front of the deck, straining to see what the lookout saw. Sure enough, she could catch glimpses of small flickering lights at the shore. Lanterns from houses.

From Arendelle.

She breathed a sigh of relief. She didn't think she'd ever been so glad to see her hometown—and that was saying something. (Though "see" might not have been the right word in this case, considering how dark the shore was as the ships pulled closer.) Elsa had lost track of time at this point and had no idea whether they were traveling in the dead of night—or the middle of the day.

"Arendelle," a voice whispered beside her as the kingdom came into view. "I never thought I'd lay eyes on it again."

Elsa turned to see that Inger had joined her at the front of the boat. Like her granddaughter, the woman had her sea legs and stood without holding on to the sides. She'd chosen to travel with them on their ship, while her granddaughter helmed the main pirate ship.

"I'm sure it doesn't bring back good memories for you," Elsa said apologetically to the former princess.

"It doesn't—and yet, in a way it does," Inger confessed, tears misting her bright blue eyes. "It was the last place I spent time with Sissel. We'd come here a lot as children. And we always had a good time in Arendelle. The people were so warm and welcoming. And the chocolate!" She licked her cracked lips. "I always loved the chocolate!"

"Sounds like you and I have a lot in common," Anna said gently, coming up beside them. She still looked a little green from the storm, but she also looked very relieved to see the shore coming closer. Inger smiled warmly at her.

"Perhaps. But you are much braver than I ever was," she told Anna. "From what I've heard, you had the courage to act. To break the dam and free the forest. The good you have done for our world cannot be overstated."

Anna blushed. "It was the right thing to do."

"Sometimes doing the right thing is the hardest thing of all," Inger replied. She stared at Arendelle's shores, looking wistful. Elsa's heart went out to her. Most of Inger's life had been spent on the run. Away from her home and her family, and without her sister. That could have easily been Elsa's fate, too, had Anna not refused to give up on her. She couldn't imagine facing the world without her sister by her side.

The sailors shouted to one another as they pulled into port. Though the storm was finally easing, it wasn't easy docking in such choppy waters, and their first tries had the ships slamming hard against the docks, causing everyone to stumble. Gale took over, easing the ships toward the land, and at last the sailors were able to jump out and tie them off.

Elsa stepped toward the gangplank once they'd given the all clear. "Come on," she said to her sister and Inger. "Let's do this."

They started down the gangplank and off the ship. But then—

"Stop! In the name of Arendelle!"

Elsa startled as a tall figure stepped before them, blocking their path. It was Mattias, and he was surrounded by guards. He pulled his sword from its sheath and pointed it at her throat.

"Who are you and why do you breach our shores? Are you pirates? For we do not suffer pirates lightly in this noble town."

Elsa stared at him in shock. Then realization fell over her.

He didn't remember her.

He didn't remember any of them!

"Mattias!" she cried in horror. "It's me! Elsa!"

"Elsa?" His lips formed her name, but there was no recognition in his eyes. "I don't know an Elsa." He turned to the guards. "Anyone here know an Elsa?"

They looked at one another, completely confused. Oh no! Their memories were gone! All of them!

"Excuse me! Coming through!"

Elsa looked behind Mattias to find Olaf trying to make his way through the crowd of soldiers. To Elsa's surprise, he was wearing a very fancy cravat and embroidered vest.

"Olaf! What on earth?" Anna started. But Olaf put a finger to his lips.

"Shh," he whispered. "Just go with it, okay?"

He leapt onto a nearby boulder and turned to face the confused citizens and soldiers. "It's all right!" he cried. "These are my friends, Elsa and Anna. They're here to help us!"

To Elsa's relief, Mattias nodded. "I'm sorry, Your

Majesty," he said. "I didn't realize." He sheathed his sword and bowed reverently to . . . Olaf?

The snowman giggled, as if embarrassed. "It's a long story," he whispered to Elsa as the crowd began to wander away. "Let's just say their memories have gotten way worse. In fact, they forgot all about you two."

"I noticed," Elsa said dryly.

"It started getting really crazy. People were fighting. No one remembered what laws were. I needed to figure out a way to keep the peace. So . . . I might have told a little story."

"That you were their ruler?" Anna asked, raising an eyebrow.

"Let's just say it worked!!" He grinned proudly. "They listened to me, and the castle and village are still standing."

"That was actually really smart," Elsa said, patting Olaf's head. "Thank you."

"I live to serve!" he declared. "But now I'm hoping you figured out a way to get out of this mess, because no one even remembers how to hug anymore! It's so sad!"

"We think so. But we need everyone's attention," Anna said. "Can you make sure they all gather at our parents' statue in the town square in the next ten minutes? We need to tell them a little story of our own."

"King Olaf at your service!" he declared. Then he shrugged sheepishly. "I mean, just leave it to me!"

Olaf scurried off, calling out orders as he went. Elsa glanced at Anna, who smiled hesitantly back at her. She knew what her sister was thinking—this had better work! Or Anna'd be ruling behind the scenes for the foreseeable future!

Elsa turned back to Inger, who was still standing on the gangplank, suddenly looking very nervous. "Are you all right?" she asked.

"I just . . . I guess I'm scared," Inger said slowly. "It's been so many years. What if they don't believe me? What if they say I should be locked up?"

"*We* believe you," Anna assured her. "And they will, too, once they hear the whole story."

"We also have Stig to back you up," Elsa added, her eyes searching the square. Had Stig made it to Arendelle? She didn't see any sign of him yet. Hopefully he hadn't gotten scared and backed out.

Inger hesitated, still looking doubtful. But her

granddaughter came up behind her, putting an arm around her shoulder.

"Come on, Gammy," she said gently. "It's time."

"I suppose you're right," Inger said. "Whatever happens, at least I can die knowing I told the truth."

Together they walked toward the town square. Olaf had done his job, and a crowd had gathered around the band's stage. Red helped her grandmother climb up the steps, and Elsa and Anna joined them, turning to the crowd.

"People of Arendelle," Anna addressed the group.

Elsa realized in dismay that no one was listening. They were all chatting with one another, not paying any attention to the people on the stage. Anna sighed, exasperated. "Olaf?" she called out. "A little help here?"

Olaf pushed through the crowd, making his way to the stage. He hopped up onto it and turned to face the crowd, putting his stick hand in his mouth and giving a loud whistle. The crowd went silent immediately. Everyone turned to the stage. Anna rolled her eyes.

"Ladies and gentlemen," Olaf said grandly. "Allow me to introduce you to your storytellers of the day! They have a fabulous tale to tell, sure to entertain you and your children. Thrills, chills, and spills galore! So please give them your undivided attention. They are my dear, dear friends, and deserve every respect."

And with that, he popped off the stage, leaving Anna, Elsa, Inger, and Red alone. Anna bit her lower lip, looking over the crowd, which was now staring up at them curiously.

"Should I start?" she whispered.

Elsa frowned. "I guess so. Though I was hoping Stig would be here. Do you see him anywhere?"

Anna scanned the crowd. "No. Do you think he backed out?"

"If he did, we're going to have a tough time proving our story."

"Do you think we should give him more time to show?"

Elsa looked up at the sky. The clouds had thickened. It looked moments away from beginning to rain again. If it started pouring, they'd lose their audience. This was their one chance.

"No. Go ahead. We'll come up with something if he doesn't appear," she told Anna.

Anna cleared her throat and turned to the people in the crowd.

"Listen up, everyone!" she said in a voice that sounded very regal, even if no one in the audience would recognize it. "As Olaf said, today we're going to tell you a story. The *true* story of Inger and Sissel. Also known as the Vesterland sisters."

The crowd clapped politely. A few small children settled up front, sitting cross-legged on the ground. Elsa wondered, suddenly, if any of them even remembered the original story of the Vesterland sisters at this point, seeing as they'd basically forgotten everything else. But then again, maybe it would be easier if they didn't remember the false story. This way they only had to be told the truth.

Maybe this had been Sissel's plan all along. . . .

And so Anna began to tell her tale. And the crowd listened, getting more invested in the story as she went on. When Sissel went over the waterfall, there was an audible gasp from many of those listening, and Red hugged her grandmother tight as she buried her face in her granddaughter's shoulder, clearly reliving her own version of the past.

"Inger did everything she could to save her sister," Anna told the crowd as she finished. "It was an accident. Simple and true. And it would have been recorded as such had it not been for our own grandfather, King Runeard, who saw the political advantage of accusing an innocent."

She went on to explain the king's greed and deception—and his fierce desire to build the dam, even at the cost of someone's life and reputation.

"But why would everyone believe him?" asked Gretchen, the painter, when Anna paused to catch her breath. "He wasn't even there! He couldn't have known what really happened."

"They believed him because I backed up his story."

Everyone whirled around at the sound of a sudden, unexpected voice. Elsa cheered silently as she caught a glimpse of the figure at the back of the crowd. Stig! He *had* come after all! And just in time, too.

"I was the witness," he said, hobbling toward the stage. People stepped back, allowing him space. He was breathing heavily and walking with a pronounced limp, but eventually he made it to the bottom of the platform.

He spotted Inger and bowed his head in shame. "I am so sorry, Princess," he said. "He threatened me, yes, but that is no excuse for my behavior. Or for hiding the truth all these years. You did not deserve what I did to you. I have lived my whole life regretting that decision."

For a moment, Inger stared down at him sternly, her blue eyes seeming to pierce into his very soul. Then her wrinkled face softened. She reached out and placed a hand on his shoulder. "I understand," she said slowly. "You were a victim as much as I was. We were practically children back then. Pawns in a deadly political game. If you did not comply, King Runeard would have likely killed you and found someone else to lie in your place. He wanted me gone, and he would have stopped at nothing to make it happen."

"Such a bad guy!" Anna grumbled. "I can't believe we're related to him!"

"Then you . . ." Stig swallowed hard. "You . . . forgive me?"

Inger nodded solemnly. "I forgive you. And I hope you will forgive yourself one day, too." The two clasped hands.

The crowd cheered excitedly. They might not have known the whole story, but they were clearly engaged. Elsa sighed. Well, she'd take what she could get.

"So now you know," Anna declared, turning back to the people of Arendelle, "the true story of the Vesterland sisters. And why greed, lies, and self-interest can never be tolerated in our kingdom again. From this day forward, their story will be written honestly in the annals of history and spread throughout the lands. Inger is not a murderer. She is a warrior. A champion of the environment. And a girl who loved her sister."

Everyone in the audience applauded and cheered. Inger stared down at them, shaking her head in disbelief.

"After all these years," she whispered. "I never thought . . ."

"Oh, Gammy!" Red hugged her tightly.

Elsa looked over the crowd, biting her lower lip. Had it worked? They'd told the true story. Did this mean everyone had their memories back?

"Mattias?" she tried, calling out to the general. But he was too busy bowing to Olaf.

Elsa turned to Anna, her face ashen. "It didn't work!" she cried. "Why didn't it work?"

"I don't know!" Anna looked as distraught as Elsa felt. "Is there something more? What else could Sissel want?"

She was interrupted by a piercing inhuman scream.

Lightning flashed across the sky, followed by the boom of thunder. A scream rang out from the direction of the harbor. Everyone turned to look, gasping in horror at what they saw.

The draugr had emerged from the depths of the sea. Slowly she crawled out of the water, covered in black seaweed, her misshapen feet squelching in the mud. Reaching the shore, she rose to her full height, her bloodshot eyes flashing with fire. She raised her arms. A low moan escaped her lips.

"Oh, my!" Inger whispered hoarsely, clinging to her granddaughter. "Is that? That can't be her! She's . . . she's—"

"A monster!" cried Helmut, grabbing his ice pick and holding it protectively in front of him. "Everyone run! Hide!"

The crowd started screaming, taking off in all directions. Sissel roared, stumbling after them.

"*Sisssssster,*" she moaned. "*SISSSSSSSTER.*"

"Wait! Stop!" Anna cried, but no one listened to her. They were too busy fleeing.

Suddenly, Mattias leapt in front of the draugr, his sword ripped from its sheath. He took a step forward, his eyes locked on the creature. His mouth pressed into a fierce frown.

"Stop in the name of Arendelle!" he commanded. "Or I will slash you down where you stand!"

"No!" Inger cried, horrified. "Please don't hurt her!"

"Mattias!" Anna tried. But he didn't even turn around. He didn't answer to her anymore. And Olaf—where was Olaf? Her eyes darted around the square, spotting the snowman trying to calm a small boy across the way. He was too far—he'd never get there in time.

Mattias charged. Elsa reacted quickly, raising her hand and shooting a wall of ice in his direction. He bounced off the ice, falling backward and landing hard on the ground. Elsa winced. She'd have to apologize later, but she couldn't let Mattias hurt Inger's sister.

"*Sissssterrr. Minnneeee . . .*"

Elsa clutched Inger's arm. "Talk to her," she urged. "She's your sister. You're the only one who can stop this!"

Inger nodded slowly, sucking in a breath. For a

moment, she no longer looked like an elderly lady, but the Pirate Queen of legends. She took a step forward, shrugging out of her granddaughter's arms. Her shoulders squared and Elsa felt a chill run down her spine.

"Sissel!"

The draugr stopped in her tracks, head cocking to the side. She turned to the source of the voice, her decaying face filled with sudden confusion.

"*Sisssssster?*" the draugr murmured.

Inger dropped off the podium and into the creature's direct line of sight. "Yes," she said, her voice quaking now. "I am your sister. Inger. And you need to stop this. Now."

Sissel let out a small moan. She stared at Inger, squinting her eyes, as if trying to determine if she was being fooled. Obviously, Inger looked nothing like the girl she had been the last time Sissel had seen her. It'd been so many years. Would the draugr recognize her?

"It's okay, Sissel," Inger whispered. "You found me. You can finally rest."

Sissel let out another moan, but this one sounded different. Not sad this time. Not angry. Not confused. But rather filled with joy.

"*Sisssster?*" she questioned. "*Sisssster mine?*"

"Yes," Inger agreed, her voice choking on the word. "Yes! You're my sister. My beloved sister. I've missed you so much."

Suddenly, to Elsa's astonishment, the draugr seemed to fade away. There was a gasp from the crowd as the creature disappeared. In its place was a ghostly vision of a young woman, dressed in old-fashioned clothes, her hair cut in a short bob.

It was Sissel, as she had appeared in life. Standing before them now.

"Inger!" Sissel cried. "Oh, Inger!"

Inger ran forward as if she were twenty years old herself. Elsa knew she was going to try to throw her arms around her sister. Heart breaking and thinking fast, Elsa shot a blast of ice in the apparition's direction, solidifying her body as best she could so that at least the two could reunite, if only for a moment. Inger reached Sissel, embracing her hard, burying her face in her icy shoulder as the whole village watched in awe.

"Oh, Sissel. I've found you at last. I've missed you so much!"

"I've missed you, too. They said terrible things about

you." Sissel's true voice had returned, sounding once again as it had in Elsa's visions. "They claimed that you murdered me. That you pushed me in the river. I tried to tell them—you would never hurt me! We're sisters, after all!"

"I know," Inger said, pulling away from the embrace. Her face was stained with tears. "But we don't have to worry about that anymore. Thanks to these two brave girls." She gestured to Elsa and Anna. "These sisters. Thanks to them, no one will ever tell our story wrong again."

Sissel's gaze traveled to the two sisters. "Thank you," she whispered. "Thank you for setting things right. And for reuniting me with my sister. You can't know how much that means to me."

"Oh, I think I have an idea," Elsa said with a small smile. She lifted her hand to her cheek, realizing it was wet with happy tears. Anna put an arm around her waist. She didn't speak, but Elsa knew exactly what she was thinking.

There was nothing in the world like the love of two sisters.

"Well," Anna declared, turning to Elsa as the sisters

tearfully embraced again. "Guess we finally figured out what Sissel wanted. You know, we probably should have guessed from the start. I mean, who doesn't want their sister back?"

Elsa smiled at her. "Who indeed," she agreed.

"Hey!" Olaf suddenly butted between them. "Look! The sun is back!"

Wait, what? Elsa's eyes shot toward the sky. She'd been so wrapped up in the happy reunion she hadn't noticed how much it had lightened outside. Now she could see that the storm clouds had rolled away, revealing a setting sun, a hazy blue twilight, and a sea of shining stars. Her breath caught in her throat.

The storm was over. Which meant . . .

She turned back to the two sisters. But to her surprise, only Inger stood there now. Sissel had vanished. Inger hobbled over to the girls, a sad smile on her face.

"She's gone," she told them. "She vanished the second the clouds went away and the sun came out."

"I'm sorry," Elsa said, laying a hand on the old pirate's arm.

"Don't be." Inger's blue eyes were wet but bright as

she looked from Elsa and Anna to Red. "You gave me something I longed for all my life. A chance to say a real goodbye. And Sissel—well, thanks to you, she's finally able to find eternal peace."

"I'm so glad," Anna said. "And I promise you now, no one will ever tell your story wrong again. We will create a monument! No, a memorial! And we can even have Wael write an article for the *Village Crown*!" she added excitedly "We will tell the whole story—exactly how it really happened! And we can spread the papers far and wide so everyone from all the surrounding kingdoms—including Vesterland—will know the truth at last."

"That sounds wonderful," Inger said. "Thank you, sweet ones. You have something of your grandmother in you, I think." She gave them a loving look.

"I wish we had known her," Anna said wistfully.

"Someday I will return and tell you all about her," Inger promised. "But for now, I must get back to my crew. They're going to want to know what's next. We've been on our mission for so long. But now we have a chance for a new beginning."

"Are you sure you can't stay?" Anna asked. "You

could join us for the Polar Nights festivities if you like. You and your crew. Arendelle will always be a home for you, if you need it."

"I appreciate that. But I have another task that must be done first." She bit her lower lip, looking a little apprehensive. "I must finally go home."

"Home to Vesterland?" Elsa asked, surprised. Though maybe she shouldn't have been.

Inger nodded. "It's been fifty years. I'd like to see it again before I die."

"That's a great idea," Anna agreed. "I can send advance word to King Jonas and his daughter, Mari," she said eagerly. "I'm sure they'd welcome you with open arms, now that the true story is known."

"Thank you," Inger said, bowing low to the two sisters. "And now, with your permission, I'll take my leave. You probably have a lot to do to clean up this whole mess." She gave a wry grin. "But I'm not worried. After all, there's nothing two sisters can't do if they put their minds to it."

Elsa turned to Anna. They both grinned. "Now that's a true story," she declared.

Anna linked arms with Elsa and watched as Inger

and her granddaughter boarded their pirate ship and prepared to set sail. The sea was now calm and the sky a beautiful blue. Sissel's hold on Arendelle was no more.

"Oh, no!" cried someone behind them. "No, no, no!"

CHAPTER TWENTY

Anna

ELSA AND ANNA EXCHANGED LOOKS. What now? They turned around, surprised to see Helmut standing in front of his block of ice, looking upset.

"What's wrong?" Elsa asked.

"My ice sculptures! I haven't even started them yet!" he cried in dismay. "How am I going to get them carved in time for the Polar Nights festival?"

"And my banner!" Gretchen burst in then, looking up at the half-blank canvas hanging haphazardly over the town square. "It's not even close to being finished."

"My waffle batter better be okay!" grumbled Bjorn. "There's no way I'm letting Bjarne win this year!"

"Oh, I'm going to win!" Bjarne broke in. "If I can find any eggs, that is. How did I forget to get eggs?" He smacked his hand to his forehead in dismay.

"It's okay!" Anna cried, leaping back onto the stage and addressing the crowd. She was shaking, she was so happy—everyone's memories were being restored! "It's all okay. We had a little setback on the Polar Nights celebration, but it doesn't matter."

"But we're not going to be ready in time!" Mrs. Blodget protested. "The party will be ruined!"

"We really wanted it to be special for you," added Halima, wringing her hands together. "We know how much it means to you. We didn't want to let our queen down."

Anna shook her head, a smile crossing her face. "You didn't let me down. Don't you understand? None of this matters! Not the ice sculptures or banners or waffles—or even chocolate. The only thing we need for a Polar Nights party is . . ." She paused dramatically. "Each other."

The crowd cheered. The Waffle Brothers hugged each other. The band grabbed their instruments and began to play a cheery tune, and the children began to dance up and down the streets. Anna threw a smile at Elsa, who smiled back even wider. Anna could tell her sister approved of her message.

Soon the village was bustling with activity. Even as the sun slipped below the horizon, people moved tables in preparation of the upcoming celebration. They hung decorations. The smell of waffle batter began to permeate the air. A farmer started to roast corn while the fishmonger started grilling thick cuts of cod. Street vendors set up stands overflowing with their wares. And was that Oaken rolling into town on a shiny new sleigh, dressed in a festive red coat and matching hat and loaded up with Polar Nights party kits?

"Hope I'm not too late!" he cried, slipping off his sleigh and hugging his family. They jumped up and down in joy to see him. "Big winter blowout!" he called out, handing a kit to an eager young child. "Free of charge!"

As the people worked, Anna could hear snippets of conversation as they busily moved around her. "Remember the story of the Vesterland sisters? Inger's innocent! Did you hear?" said one. "That awful King Runeard! How dare he force that poor shepherd to lie!"

said another. "Our dear Queen Rita was Inger's savior. Can you believe it?" said a third. The true story spread far and wide.

There was just one thing missing. One thing to make this a truly happily ever after. Anna turned to Elsa. "Can I send Gale on a little mission?" she asked hesitantly. "Would you mind?"

"Already done," Elsa assured her. "And Gale's fast. I bet it's already reached the trolls. And a certain ice harvester." She winked at her sister.

Anna's heart leapt in her chest as she thought of Kristoff. Her Kristoff. She couldn't wait to throw her arms around him and squeeze him so tight he'd squeak. She'd have to decide later whether she'd ever let him go.

"Queen Anna?"

She turned to see Wael approaching her, quill and paper in hand. "Do you have a moment? I'd love to interview you for the *Village Crown*. A front-page story above the fold this time. With a big picture! All about how you saved Arendelle from Sinister Sissel and—"

"Actually? Sissel wasn't sinister," Olaf broke in, waddling up behind the reporter. He had taken off his cravat and looked much more comfortable *au natural.* "In fact, she was actually kind of sweet."

"You're right! I saw it with my own eyes. I should have known better than to call her that. I'm sorry, she's Sweet Sissel." Wael wrote it down in his notebook. "See, this is why I need the interview. I want to make sure I get it exactly right."

"I can help with that," Olaf assured him, giving Anna a knowing look. "Let's let our queen do her job and you can interview me instead. After all, I'm the only one around this place who never forgot a thing. I'm the true witness!"

"As am I," Stig chimed in, walking up to the snowman and reporter. "And it's time I tell my tale, officially. Once and for all."

Wael rubbed his hands together excitedly. "Well, this is great!" he exclaimed. "You two can tell me everything! But we must hurry. The paper must go to press within the hour so I can get the issue out in time for the festivities."

"Wael?" Anna said suddenly. "I might need a bonus edition of the paper after the festival is done." She looked at her sister. "I need to reach out to King Jonas of Vesterland about this, but I feel like Inger and Sissel need a proper memorial, too. Not that overgrown run-down one. We will want everyone's help getting it ready. Maybe even before Inger sets sail again?"

Elsa smiled. "That sounds like a wonderful idea."

"Bonus issue! Of the *Village Crown*!" Wael repeated. "Yes, my queen! So much to do! I'm on it!"

He hurried Olaf and Stig off. Anna watched them go, amused. Olaf was already talking Wael's ear off.

"I wonder if Stig will manage to get a word in edgewise," she remarked to Elsa. Her sister snorted.

"Poor Stig," she said.

"Poor Wael," Anna added.

They started to laugh. It felt good to laugh again after such a harrowing few days of thinking she'd lost everything. Including her own memories. She closed her eyes and started cataloging her thoughts, searching for any holes. But everything seemed intact.

"That's it, then," she sighed happily. "We did it. We saved Arendelle."

"Once more with feeling," Elsa said. "You know, this is getting to be a bit of a habit."

"This has got to be the last time," Anna declared. She frowned. "You think it's the last time, right?"

"Oh, yes. Definitely." Elsa gave her a teasing grin.

Anna poked her playfully. "I do hope Inger decides to come visit someday," she said. "I'd love to hear more about her and Sissel. And our grandmother, too."

Before Elsa could answer, there was a rumble, so loud it almost sounded like an earthquake. Everyone in the village stopped what they were doing and turned to see what looked like a dozen or more boulders rolling and bouncing down the village street. They tumbled to a stop in front of Anna and Elsa and sprang into the air, transforming into the trolls Anna knew so well. The largest boulder rolled forward, stopping at the front of the group. The rock flipped over to reveal Grand Pabbie.

"Your Majesties," Grand Pabbie said in that deep voice of his. This time there was a smile on his rocky face. "You succeeded in saving the Polar Nights and helping a draugr find eternal rest. Well done! Arendelle's future is secure once more."

A cheer rose up around the trolls, but Anna still felt restless. She wouldn't feel complete until . . . "Kristoff?" she asked hurriedly, searching behind all the trolls. It was the longest they'd been apart since . . . well, ever. She missed him so much. Had he gotten his memories back, too?

"ANNA!"

And suddenly there he was. Speeding over the bridge and into the village, on the back of Sven, who was going so fast that for a moment she mistook him for the Water Nokk.

Her eyes welled with tears. He was not only here, but he had said her name. He had said her name because he remembered her name.

"KRISTOFF!" she cried, taking off running.

Whisk! Anna felt the wind at her back and realized Gale was there, helping her reach her fiancé quicker. Within seconds, they were together. Finally!

"Anna," Kristoff said, practically jumping off Sven's back. Sven greeted Anna with a lick on her cheek, but that was nothing compared to Kristoff's greeting. He pulled her straight into his arms and up into the air, spinning her around before finally placing her back on the ground and kissing her deeply. He cupped her face. "Are you all right? I feel like I haven't seen you in days! No, weeks!" He shook his head. "I feel like my head was in a fog, but now it's lifting, and the minute it did, I looked at Sven and said—'Anna! We have to get to Anna and see what she needs!' So? Are you all right?"

"Am I all right?" Anna cried, laughing through her tears. "Are you? Who am I?" she demanded. "Tell me quickly!"

Kristoff blinked at her before his face broke into a huge smile. "You're my feisty, fearless, ginger-sweet fiancée."

She threw her arms around him again. "You're back!"

"I'm back," he said, holding her tightly. "And if I'm not mistaken, I believe today is our Choco-versary."

"YES!" Anna practically shouted with relief. Then she blushed and added, "But it's been a rough few days. All that matters is we're together again."

"Please. Do you think I'd forget our Choco-versary?" Kristoff scoffed. "What kind of fiancé do you think I am?"

He whistled, and Sven, who had wandered off without Anna's knowledge, returned, balancing a large box on his back. Kristoff ran over and grabbed the top of the box. "Happy Choco-versary, my love! Ta-da!"

The witnessing trolls all cheered.

Anna's heart felt as if it would burst out of her chest as she pulled the box cover off, revealing a giant . . . wait, what was that?

"Um, is that a chocolate Flemmingrad the fungus troll?" she asked, her eyes bulging.

"Oh my," Mattias said, loud enough for everyone to hear.

"Yes! I quickly made him out of mushroom-flavored chocolate and edible plants!" Kristoff said excitedly, plucking a strange-looking purple leaf out of the troll's ear and popping it into his mouth. "Yum! Delicious! Should I break off a piece for you?"

"Uh, that's okay," Anna said, backing up slightly. "We should probably . . . um . . . wait until my gift for you is ready!" she finished brightly.

"Oh, my dear, but it is!" said Mrs. Blodget as she popped out of her shop, carrying the large reindeer-shaped chocolate Anna had commissioned weeks before. She couldn't believe Mrs. Blodget even had it done after all that had happened.

Anna smiled sheepishly at Kristoff. "Happy Choco-versary?" she said.

"Amazing!" Kristoff declared, looking right at her.

And she was pretty sure he wasn't just talking about the chocolate. A warm, gooey feeling fell over her, and she reached for his hand.

"I love you," she whispered.

"I love you, too," he said. "And don't you forget it."

She snorted. "To be fair, I'm not the one who—"

Her words were interrupted by a low *ooh*. Followed by a group *ahh*. She turned from Kristoff to see what it was.

"Look!" said Mattias. "It's the Northern Lights!"

A hush came over the village. Everyone looked up into the sky, murmuring excitedly at the shafts of greens and golds whisking across the horizon like a nighttime rainbow. The aurora borealis. Here at last. Anna felt a shiver trip down her spine. She cuddled a little closer to Kristoff, putting her head on his shoulder.

"It's so beautiful," she whispered. "So perfect."

Kristoff put an arm around her, and Olaf jumped into Elsa's arms. Sven came up alongside them, and Anna scratched him behind the ears. All around them, the Arendellians looked up in awe at the spectacular show in the sky.

"You wanted the best Polar Nights ever," Elsa said,

leaning in to whisper in Anna's ear. "I'm pretty sure you got it."

"Yes," Anna agreed. "This is definitely a night I won't soon forget."

CHAPTER TWENTY-ONE

Anna

Two Weeks Later . . .

It was amazing how different a place felt when sadness was replaced with hope.

Standing near the river at the border of Vesterland and Arendelle where Sissel had lost her life, Anna marveled at how much had been done in such a short amount of time.

The tiny makeshift memorial area had been cleared of overgrown weeds and shrubs to make way for a larger space with a hand-carved canopy and natural rock seating (Kristoff's idea), along with hand-carved benches (Olga's idea) for visitors to sit at and reflect. Snow currently covered the ground, but in the spring Anna could already envision the grassy knoll and canopy filled with wildflowers (Helga said they were Sissel's favorite).

Underneath the canopy sat a veiled statue that Anna would be christening that morning alongside Elsa, King Jonas, and Princess Mari. Helmut had been working night and day over the last two weeks to complete the statue of the Vesterland sisters, whose true story had finally been told.

And for those who hadn't heard it yet, there was now a large plaque etched into rock that told the tale of Sissel and Inger and what both had strived to do for their kingdom. It also included the story of what had actually happened between them that fateful December day at the river and all that Inger had endured in the weeks that followed when she was accused of Sissel's murder.

The little wooden statue that Olga and Helga had made to serve as the original memorial hadn't been forgotten, either. It would soon reside in the Vesterland History Museum along with a new exhibit about Sissel and Inger that Mari was overseeing with Olga and Helga's help. Anna couldn't imagine anyone better suited to tell Sissel and Inger's story than their loyal stewards. Well, other than Inger herself.

Anna felt a cool hand on her shoulder; she didn't have to ask who was there. "Do you think she's going to show?" Anna asked Elsa without turning to look at her.

"I'm not sure," Elsa said thoughtfully, staring at the rushing river just a few feet away. For safety's sake, Anna insisted the grounds of the memorial now include a wooden fence to keep others from falling in when they visited the site. "It might be too painful for her to come back here again."

Anna hadn't spoken to Inger since that day at the festival. When she had met with the pirates to discuss a new trade agreement, Red was the one who had done the negotiating on Inger's behalf. And now that a peace deal had been brokered, Red had sent word to Anna that the pirates would be leaving the fjord in a few days' time. Anna's invitation to join them today at the memorial ceremony had gone unanswered.

"You don't think Inger is afraid to meet with the people of Vesterland, do you?" Elsa wondered.

"Red said Inger was hoping to meet privately with

Jonas and Mari. I'm sure they assured her she's welcome in her homeland again." Anna looked around at all the people putting the finishing touches on things before the ceremony. Arendellians and the people of Vesterland had worked overtime to bring the memorial site together so quickly. Now, people from both kingdoms were tying blue and purple ribbons, which happened to be Sissel and Inger's favorite colors, around all the chairs at the service and weaving handmade silk flowers into the canopy covering the statue. "I just want her to be here so she can see for herself how much she and Sissel mean to everyone. Today is their celebration."

"Seriously!" Olaf said, bounding up to them with both a blue silk flower and a purple one. "When was the last time we had two parties to plan in two weeks?" He placed one of his tree-branch arms across his forehead. "I'm exhausted from planning!"

"Party pooper," Kristoff teased as he and Sven joined the others. "All you had to do was spread the word about the memorial. It's not like you had to transport heavy rocks to the site and carve a wooden canopy like me and Sven."

Anna stood on tippy-toes to kiss him. "It all looks

great, honey. I can't imagine a better tribute to the Vesterland sisters."

"The next party I throw will be your and Kristoff's engagement party," Olaf said. "Sven and I already have a theme planned. Right, Sven?" Sven snorted.

"Give me a little time off to rest first," Kristoff said, speaking on his reindeer's behalf. "I'm still recovering from the Polar Nights festival."

"That's good, because I want a say on that party theme, too," Elsa teased and looked at Anna. "It's too bad you can't plan your own engagement party. You did such a great job with the Polar Nights."

Anna blushed as Kristoff put his arm around her and pulled her close.

"I second that! It was the best one ever, I'll have you know." He blanched. "No offense to our snow queen."

Elsa laughed. "None taken!"

Anna blushed. "Thanks, everyone. Considering half the village couldn't remember who they were for most of the planning stage, things came together rather nicely at the end."

"Only because they have a great leader to help get things done," Elsa reminded her.

"A leader who is good at delegating!" Anna said with a small fist pump. "Which is what I'm going to do now to make sure this ceremony is perfect." She looked out at the crowd of people again and prayed she'd spot Inger or the pirates. She didn't.

Kristoff gave her another squeeze as the gray day gave way to peeks of sun through the clouds. "Cheer up. Even if the pirates don't come today, I'm sure they appreciate what you've done here. And something tells me Sissel is somewhere watching."

"Just not as a draugr, right?" Olaf looked momentarily alarmed.

"Actually, I like to imagine Sissel almost like Gale— just a lovely afternoon wind gliding by on its way to see the world now that it can," Elsa offered. Olaf looked appeased.

The sound of horses approaching in the distance announced King Jonas's arrival. His carriage came to a stop near the clearing and he stepped out, walking straight over to Anna and Elsa.

"Queens Anna and Elsa," he said, clasping their hands as Mari walked over to join them. "I'm so glad we could do this today, and so quickly! Thank you for all your help the past few weeks."

"Vesterland and Arendelle are not only allies and neighbors, we're friends," Anna reminded the king. "Nothing could mean more to Elsa and me than the chance to make things right."

"Good. Because we brought a few extra friends along to celebrate." Mari stepped aside, gesturing with her hands. Anna watched in surprise as the crowd parted to make way for a familiar-looking band of pirates.

"They came!" Olaf said, jumping up and down.

Anna couldn't believe her eyes. The pirates had come after all, and they were all dressed for the occasion in their finest boots and leather vests, hats with feathers atop their heads, each one wearing a blue ribbon for Sissel woven into their hair or tied to their vest. Red led the way, holding the arm of her grandmother, Inger, whose attendance was the biggest surprise of all. Anna watched as Old Blue Eyes took in the scene around her with wonder. Inger blinked away tears, but she was smiling. In her hands, she held tight to a bouquet of wildflowers— the same flowers that were woven through the two long white braids in her hair. Where Inger had found them in the winter, Anna had no idea.

"Good to see you, both," Inger said with a small nod. "We hope we're not too late."

"Late? Never! We couldn't start without you," said Anna as she clasped Inger's hands and didn't let go. "We're glad you're here. It's so good to see you again."

"And you two as well," Inger said with a soft smile. "This place has been transformed. It looks so peaceful. Sissel would be pleased."

"She's . . . at peace?" Kristoff couldn't help asking.

"Yes," Inger said, exhaling softly. "We both are. My sister's spirit is now free, and so am I. It's back to the sea I go with my family." She tightened her grip on Red's arm.

"We hope you know you're welcome in Vesterland anytime," King Jonas told Inger. "It is your homeland, after all."

"We could find you a place, help you settle back in," Mari added. "There are so many people here who miss you and want to see you again." She looked over at Olga and Helga, who were hugging and crying at the same time at the sight of Inger.

Inger took one look at her former stewards and her

tears flowed harder. "Thank you. And I do appreciate the generous offer. It's been so long since I've stood on dry land for any amount of time." She looked at Red. "But the sea is where I want to spend my remaining years. It is truly my home now, but it's not everyone's. My granddaughter should have the chance to have a real life in Vesterland."

King Jonas cleared his throat. "Of course, and as a descendant of the royal family, Red could also lay claim to the—"

"I'll stop you right there, King Jonas," interrupted Red. "While I appreciate the offer to reclaim my family's royal line, I'm truly like my grandmother." She looked at the older woman. "I am a pirate and I belong at sea, not in a castle." The two embraced. "But it is good to know there is somewhere I can call home if ever I tire of the water."

King Jonas nodded. "You will always have a place here."

"We hope you'll make this memorial space your own and visit often. Vesterland even has plans for an exhibit about you and Sissel in their museum," Mari informed her.

"Is that right?" Inger said. "I hope Olga and Helga are helping put that together. They have such wonderful stories about our childhood, and even our nicknames." She chuckled. "Sissel hated how we all called her 'Stinky Sissel' when she ate too much garlic."

Everyone laughed.

"Noted!" said Elsa.

Olaf giggled loudest of all. "Stinky Sissel is a much better nickname than—"

"Don't say Sinister Sissel!" Anna cut him off. "Well, if you're all ready, it's time." Anna took Inger's free arm and led her and Red to the front of the waiting crowd by the bench.

By now, everyone was holding candles that were lit one by one. King Jonas, Mari, and Elsa moved to the front, where Anna joined them, looking out on all the people who had gathered for this important moment in their kingdoms' shared history. Her eyes were on Inger's.

"Thank you all for coming today to help us unveil the Vesterland sisters' memorial," Anna said.

"Their true story is long overdue," continued Jonas. "And it is the hope of both Vesterland and Arendelle that people will come to this memorial site often to reflect on both sisters' lives and what they did for their kingdom."

Anna moved to the sheet covering the statue. "And now, may we present, this memorial statue—*The Love of Two Vesterland Sisters* by Master Sculptor Helmut of Arendelle."

She and Kristoff pulled the sheet away, revealing a hand-carved statue of Sissel and Inger in a tight embrace. They were carved as their younger selves, looking vibrant and hopeful as they stared into one another's eyes. *This is the way the world should remember them,* Anna thought, *as a united front; two sisters who fought together for the betterment of Vesterland and who loved each other till their dying days; a young woman lost far too soon and the sister who loved her so much that she spent her life searching for her.*

Inger let out a small gasp at the sight of her younger self with Sissel, then rose and made her way slowly to the statue. Her granddaughter did the same, both of them touching the smooth stone and looking at it in wonder.

"Do you like it?" Anna asked shyly, her hand moving to find Elsa's.

Inger looked at both queens with love in her teary eyes. "It's perfect. Absolutely perfect."

And just at that moment, a sudden gust of wind rustled through the bare trees, blowing the last of the autumn leaves through the knoll with such force that people held on to their hats and gasped in surprise.

Anna felt a smile come to her lips. She looked at Elsa, remembering her sister's words from earlier.

Sissel.

She was there, and she was finally at peace.

CHAPTER TWENTY-TWO

Elsa

"WHAT A DAY!" ANNA DECLARED as she collapsed onto Elsa's bed in a dramatic swoon. She had changed into her favorite green nightgown and had taken her hair out of its braids. *She looks younger like this,* Elsa thought. As if she were still that little girl, begging Elsa to build a snowman.

Instead, she was a queen who had saved her kingdom.

Well, with a little help from her older sister, of course.

"Cuddle close, scooch in," Elsa joked, pulling her sister to her. Anna lay her head on her shoulder, sighing happily.

"I didn't think we could pull it off," Anna murmured,

cozying up to her sister. "I really didn't. But in the end everyone came through."

"A Polar Nights and a memorial celebration," Elsa declared. "Not to mention my epic birthday surprise! It's been quite a few weeks. Ones hopefully everyone will remember for years to come. I know I definitely will."

Anna sighed dreamily. "Ah, memories. So glad to have those back."

"Agreed," Elsa concurred. "I stopped by Ahtohallan on the way back from the memorial, and everything seemed back to normal. I was able to pull up all the usual memories. It was nice seeing them again, let me tell you."

"I bet," Anna said wistfully. "I wish I could see for myself."

"Well . . ." Elsa sat up in bed, her eyes shining with eagerness. "Actually, I have a little gift for you."

"Gift? But it was just your birthday, not mine."

"Oh, shush and let me share," Elsa scolded. She gave her sister a mysterious grin, then closed her eyes, picturing the memory she'd pulled from Ahtohallan just for this occasion. Then she pushed out her hands, sending it through her fingers. When she opened her eyes, she saw a swirl of icy wind, whirling in the middle of the bedroom, forming moving shapes.

"Oh my goodness! It's our parents. Are they on the ship?" asked Anna, mouth agape.

Elsa watched breathlessly as the scene unfolded: their mother and father, standing in some kind of ship's cabin.

Mother's eyes were filled with tears. *"Maybe we made a mistake isolating them. Maybe we should have—"*

"We did what we thought was best," their father said firmly. *"Only time will tell if it was right or wrong. But I have faith in them. They are young, but they are already so strong. And if anyone can help Elsa, it's Anna."* He smiled softly. *"There's not much that girl can't do."*

"You're right about that," their mother replied, shaking her head. *"Her love could hold up the world."*

Their father nodded. *"When the time comes, I truly believe they will do the right thing."*

"For Arendelle?"

"No." Their father shook his head. *"For each other."*

And with that, the shimmery vision faded, the ice dissolving into the air. For a moment, neither sister spoke. They just stared at the spot where their parents had stood. Then Elsa glanced over at Anna, catching her sister swiping a tear from her eyes.

"They really believed in us," she whispered, her voice hoarse. "The whole time."

"And they were right," Elsa told her, feeling her own voice choke up. "I would be nothing without your love."

She pulled Anna into her arms. They hugged tightly— so tightly that Elsa could barely breathe. But she didn't care. She had her sister. She had her memories. The kingdom was safe.

The sun would rise again. And life would begin anew.

Suddenly the door banged open. The sisters turned to see Olaf, accompanied by Kristoff and Sven. The snowman carried a thick book of stories in his hand. He waved it at the two sisters.

"When's our next campout?" he asked. "Because it's my turn, finally, to tell a spooky story! And I've got the best one, too! You thought the draugr was scary? Let me tell you about the dreaded Pesta, who sweeps into town on a broom, bringing pesty pestilence and plague!"

Elsa groaned. She grabbed the book out of Olaf's hand. Then she whistled for Gale to come through the open window and whisk it away. The Wind Spirit happily obliged.

"Aw! But this was such a good one!" Olaf griped as he watched the book sail through the window and disappear.

"No more scary stories," Anna scolded, wagging a finger at him. "Only happy endings from here on out!"

Elsa smiled, slinging an arm over her sister's shoulder. "Happy endings sound good to me," she agreed. "And lots of memories, shared together."

~ THE END ~

ACKNOWLEDGMENTS

THERE IS NO GREATER GIFT for two authors who adore Elsa and Anna as much as we do to be asked to tackle an all-new, original Frozen tale . . . except maybe to be asked to do it together! (Finishing each other's sandwiches!) We had more fun than we ever thought possible plotting and writing this book with our incredible editor and fellow Disney nerd, Heather Knowles, who is always full of ideas, enthusiasm, and virtual chocolate on the hard days. (Mmm . . . chocolate!) Heather, we couldn't have had a better partner in this world. We wish we could buy you your own personal sauna from Wandering Oaken's just to show you how much we care!

It takes a kingdom to write a book, and we are so lucky to have the amazing team at Disney Publishing on our side, including project manager Monica Vasquez, print production manager Anne Peters, illustrator Olga Mosqueda (for that incredibly spooky cover!), and designers Alfred Giuliani, Winnie Ho, and Susan Gerber, as well as Seale Ballenger and Lyssa Hurvitz. We wish we could give you all warm hugs. Special thanks also go to Heather Blodget from Walt Disney Animation Studios—we could pick your brain all day for Frozen lore. . . .

More thanks and a bundle of Sven's carrots go to our incredible agents, Mandy Hubbard and Dan Mandel, without whom we'd be completely lost in the woods.

And most importantly, Frozen fans—this book is for YOU. We thought of you with every sentence we wrote and can't wait for you to go "into the unknown" on this new adventure with your favorite sisters and their friends. We hope you love reading their story as much as we enjoyed writing it.

And finally, to our families—there is no place like home, and we're so thankful ours is with you!

—Mari and Jen